## "MICHAEL RAINTREE ..."

Laura rolled the syllables around in her mouth, savoring them like candy. "I like that name."

"I like that *man!*" Monica sighed. "How can anybody be that good-looking and be . . ." She paused, searching for the right word, ". . . holy."

Laura gave her a half-smile. "I don't know. But I'd sure like to find out."

"What?" Monica asked. "You can't seriously be thinking of going to that—that Mission! He's absolutely gorgeous but not worth the risk of being attacked."

"Don't be a bore," Laura chided. "I'm sure there's some kind of security . . ."

Monica kept up a steady stream of "should nots" all the way to the car. Laura nodded but ignored her. She had made up her mind. She wanted to see Michael Raintree one more time. She didn't understand why, but she knew it was important. There was something beyond his rugged good looks—something burning inside his eyes, his voice, his heart—a living fire. And she had to touch it one more time.

# ETERNAL FLAME

*Lurlene McDaniel*

**Serenade/Serenata**
BOOKS
of the Zondervan Publishing House
Grand Rapids, Michigan

ISBN 0-310-46641-3

Edited by Anne Severance
Designed by Kim Koning

*Printed in the United States of America*

85  86  87  88  89  90  /  10  9  8  7  6  5  4  3  2  1

*To all the righteous men of God*
*who daily run the race and fight*
*the good fight*

## Acknowledgments

I would like to thank my husband Joe for his support, and Monte Wilson and Bill Mikler for their ministries and invaluable input toward the writing of this book.

*PROLOGUE*

The old woman crouched, sniffed the morning air of the jungle, and sighed. Rain! The damp promising smell of rain clung to the dark green foliage like an invisible blanket. Her tribe would have to keep moving. Moving as they had been for the past many days. Moving . . . searching for a new place to build their village. A place where the rain wouldn't wash them out again.

She looked down at the palm fronds in her hardened hands. Her eyes were old and sometimes her vision blurred, but not so this morning. With great care she pulled back the outermost part of the leaves and peered at the one large glowing ember secured in the hollowed-out rock and shielded by the fronds.

A great swelling of pride filled her being. As the eldest and the most sure-footed of her people, she was entrusted with the most sacred task of all. She was the guardian of the fire. The one selected to carry the flame of immortality to the new village site. Without this burning ember, she knew that the village elders could not make a new fire.

And without a central village fire, the people could not cook the meat brought in from hunting forays by the warriors. Without fire, there would be no warmth. Without fire, there would be no way to protect the village from the predators that prowled the jungle at night.

She stared at the ember for a long time. Contact with the moist air had cooled it. She puffed gently on the surface of the grayish lump. A thin spiral of white smoke rose and filled her nostrils. Satisfied that the cinder still burned, she carefully rewrapped the fronds over the precious package. Hers was an awesome responsibility.

If she failed to keep the ember burning, the tribal chief would appoint a warrior who, at risk to his own life, must steal fire from another village. Though stealing was an ancient taboo, life was cheap in the jungle. Commodities were not.

The old woman had heard legends of vast cities set outside the boundaries of the deep forests where there was never any lack of fire—where bright and gleaming lights lit up the dark and sent a white glow far into the night skies. But she didn't believe these stories. It didn't seem possible that she could have lived all these years along the great, winding jungle river and never have seen these huge lighted cities heralded in legends and stories.

From overhead, a brilliantly plumed parrot let out a raucous cry. A group of monkeys screeched and began leaping from tree to tree like pursued thieves. The woman sighed and stood up, stretching her cramped muscles. The scouts had returned. The word had been given. It was time to move on.

The old woman squared her shoulders and clutched the palm fronds to her tightly. A sense of pride and destiny filled her. As long as she preserved it, the fire would not go out. This was her mission. Her sacred trust. She would not fail her people. The fire would be theirs forever.

Ever so softly, a fine rain began to fall. . . .

*CHAPTER 1*

"MONICA, PLEASE CHECK and see if this traffic is *ever* going to start moving again!" Laura Garland instructed her friend while she leaned impatiently on the horn of her vintage sports car. The woman seated next to her in the leather bucket seat, elevated herself and peered over the windshield of the convertible. Then she flopped noisily back down onto the car seat.

"Sorry, luv . . . it's hopeless!"

"Darn!" Laura muttered. She had been foolish to cut through the downtown area during rush hour. She gave the horn a series of staccato taps. The car in front of her refused to budge, and, through the rear-view mirror, the car behind appeared glued to her bumper. The driver, a beefy man with fat cheeks, smirked knowingly and blew her a kiss.

"Creep!" Laura muttered. Then she gunned the engine of her hot-red Thunderbird and looked for another way to circumvent the traffic jam.

"Just be patient, darling," Monica urged. "We're stuck—and there's not a thing we can do about it at the moment."

"We'll see about *that!*" Laura defiantly scanned her surroundings.

The buildings along Miami's Biscayne Boulevard cast long shadows over the sidewalks and streets in the waning afternoon sunlight. The expansive thoroughfare overflowed with five-o'clock traffic as commuters hurried to get home before nightfall. Tall, regal royal palms lined the median of the famous boulevard, standing like sentries over the whitewashed city of eternal summer.

Yet summer was only a memory on this particular afternoon. It was one of those rare Miami winter days when the morning had dawned with temperatures in the fifties. The northern breezes from a stubborn Arctic cold front had refused to allow the mercury to climb above 65 degrees all day. Laura tugged her Chanel-cut crimson suede jacket more snugly to her sides and settled on an alternate plan.

Coincidentally, she noticed that they were stranded in the southbound lane, directly across from Biscayne Park, the band shell, and the public library. "Well, we're not going to sit here and wait!" she announced firmly.

"Where do you plan to go, darling?" Monica drawled. "The moon?"

"Just watch me," she commanded.

Laura cut her wheels sharply to the left, eased up onto the median, and drove across the grassy strip, dodging a massive palm tree. With a fluid motion she slid the car into the off-street parking space that ran parallel to the park. The drivers in the line of stalled traffic watched the maneuver with interest—some with a good-natured wave; others, with a scowl of frustration.

Laura halted the car, opened the door, and stepped out gracefully, her long, silken legs attracting a few whistles from car-bound motorists. She slammed the door emphatically. "Are you coming?"

"Coming where?"

"To take a walk in the park and wait 'til this traffic clears."

"Oh, really, Laura . . . stop making such a big deal out of a little traffic jam." Monica paused. "Besides, it's cold, and you know how much I hate cold weather."

"I refuse to sit in that line when I could be doing something more productive," Laura called over her shoulder. She started off at a brisk pace and, after a few moments, heard Monica following her.

"Oh, all right," Monica said crossly as she caught up and fell into step with Laura's long-legged stride. "I'll come. It's certainly no fun sitting alone in a parked car waiting on you!"

The two women crossed over onto the clipped green lawns of the park and started toward the sea wall that restrained the swirling waters of Biscayne Bay.

"I'm thinking of letting Raul recolor my hair to more of a platinum shade," Monica said. "What do you think?" Laura shrugged and Monica added with a grumble, "Of course, you don't have to worry a twit about *your* hair. All those natural waves . . ."

"Monica, it's only hair," Laura teased, the cool air greatly reviving her spirits. "Now, wasn't this a good idea?" she asked, inhaling deeply and turning to study her friend's reaction.

"Well, I sure don't want to be here when the sun goes down." Monica refused to be pacified. "Besides, Fran's party is tonight."

"Not another stuffy little get-together at Fran's?" Laura sighed.

"*Brad* will be there."

*Hmmm, Brad Meyers might be worth the boring evening,* Laura thought. He was both handsome and eligible. A rare combination. Not that she had ever lacked for male attention. She'd always had more than any woman's fair share of attentive, even fawning, men. But Brad had been one of the few who hadn't fallen all over her when they'd first met last summer. Based on that fact alone, he was an interesting prospect.

Long shadows stretched like fingers across the paths as they walked along. From a park bench an old man, his worn trenchcoat pulled tightly over his thin frame, was feeding a flock of pigeons. At their approach the birds darted aside, too lazy to fly, too tame to flee, and reluctant to abandon, even temporarily, their handout of stale bread crumbs.

Laura breathed deeply, savoring the taste of the air, and shook her full head of honey-colored hair. It felt good to be outdoors. She'd been cooped up all day in her father's high-rise glass and chrome office building. Too much coffee and not enough lunch had left her irritable and short-tempered. Monica was right. Why should she let a little traffic jam get to her?

At twenty-five Laura had a degree in public relations from the University of Miami, her real estate license, a position as top salesperson of commercial property in her father's multimillion-dollar firm—in short, she had *everything*. Yet . . . yet . . .

Why did she feel so empty? So purposeless? Like she was just drifting through life instead of truly living it?

" . . . don't you think so?"

With a start, Laura realized that Monica had been speaking. "Sorry," she said. "My mind was wandering. What did you say?"

"I want to know if you're interested in giving Linda Collins a run for her money. Brad is adorable. At least you once thought so," Monica said.

Laura shrugged. Normally, men like Brad didn't appeal to her. She found his blond beachboy good looks a little too pretty for her tastes. But he did intrigue her in a way. "I don't know," she told

13

Monica. "The thought of suffering through Fran's party. . . ."

"So what? The two of you could cut out early."

"Ever since Fran hooked up with that phony artsy crowd of hers . . ." Laura's voice trailed away. "Can't she see how they just use her . . . *and* her father's money?"

"Fran doesn't care," Monica said. "She loves attention and has never really cared how she got it."

"Why do you want to go tonight?" Laura paused along the path and turned to face her friend.

"Nothing better to do," Monica shrugged. "I'm one of the 'idle rich,' remember?" she teased. "I don't have a high-powered career like *some* people I know."

There was an edge of bitterness in Monica's voice. Laura wondered again why she and Monica Jerrel were friends at all. They were so different. Perhaps it was just habit. They'd grown up together, gone to school together . . . their fathers even worked together. Ted Jerrel had been handling Mackenzie Garland's financial empire for years. Even before it had become one of the largest real estate concerns in South Florida. Both men were worth millions.

Yet . . . yet . . . the longings, the yearnings for something more pricked Laura more cruelly each day. And she had the vague, uneasy feeling that Brad Meyers wasn't going to be the answer.

"What do you suppose is going on over there?" Monica asked as she peered over Laura's shoulder. Laura turned to see a large, attentive crowd of people gathered at the base of the park's Torch of Freedom monument.

"I've no idea," she shrugged. "And I'm not about to find out. The last thing we need is to get tangled up in some right-wing political thing."

"Who says it's political? Come on," Monica said, tugging on Laura's elbow. "Let's go check it out."

14

"Oh, Monica . . . *really*," There was a tinge of irritation in Laura's voice. But she allowed herself to be led to the fringes of the crowd. Someone was speaking, and the speaker's voice was male, resonant and powerful. In spite of her irritation, she was curious.

Laura edged her way through the crowd, craning to see above the heads of the bystanders. She saw the man at once. His appearance was commanding, vibrantly handsome, charismatic. He stood facing the crowd, his hair black and windblown, one strand trailing over his forehead. He was tall, well over six feet, ram-rod straight. But it was his eyes that arrested her, held her. They were the color of the deep parts of the ocean on a sun-drenched afternoon, cool blue with a wash of violet, yet burning with some inner fire.

"Would you look at that . . . ?" Monica murmured appreciatively into her ear. "I don't know what party he's with, but sign me up!"

Laura appraised him, evaluated him, struggled to categorize him, to relate him to her frame of reference. He wasn't dressed like a politician. He was wearing a white turtleneck sweater, a suede jacket, Levis, and loafers. He had an air of total authority, yet the appearance of a casual friend. His penetrating eyes swept the crowd.

Then, quite suddenly, they locked onto hers with the effect of a bolt of blue lightning. An involuntary shiver went up her spine. She couldn't look away. She felt caught up, as in a maelstrom, and the magnetism in his eyes and the fire in his powerful voice drew her with invisible bonds.

Slowly, his words began to penetrate her consciousness. "Because the answer is Jesus Christ . . ." she heard him say. "And no one comes to God except through Him!"

"A *preacher?*" Monica whispered incredulously. "I can see I need to go back to church!"

But Laura only half-heard her friend. The man's eyes were boring into her, burning a hole in her mind that left a window open to her soul. It all happened in a few moments, then his gaze shifted away. But Laura felt weak in her knees. The encounter with the stranger, the preacher, the blue-eyed man, had shaken her. And she didn't know why.

"Are you all right?" Monica asked.

"Fine," Laura replied, her voice husky.

Beside the street preacher stood two other men. One had a guitar slung casually over his shoulder. The second stood holding a fistful of leaflets. Both kept their attention focused on the speaker. And the crowd was strangely quiet, too, not issuing the cat-calls and jibes so typical of street people.

Laura glanced at them from the corner of her eye. They were old and young. They were black, white, Cuban, down-and-outers . . . the fringes of humanity. Yet all were riveted to the words and persona of the speaker. Under normal conditions, Laura would never have been seen in such a crowd. Now, she couldn't help herself.

"He died for you . . ." the man was saying, "because He loved you . . . We are all sinners and deserve death. He came to give us life more abundant." His words hung in the air, heavy with meaning, eliciting a response of awed silence from the spectators.

Then the man with the leaflets stepped forward and said loudly, "If you want to hear more, take one of these." He waved the papers and the people began to reach out for them, hesitantly at first, then more eagerly, until the fellow was surrounded by grasping hands.

Laura was no different. She *had* to have a leaflet. She took one, glancing covertly at the preacher as she

16

passed him. He was listening intently to a man dressed in the uniform of poverty—dirty, ill-fitting trousers and a grayed shirt, frayed and buttonless. She felt a keen disappointment when the preacher did not notice her passing. Men had always noticed her. But this one . . . this one was different.

Clutching the paper, she joined Monica at the back of the Torch monument.

"So who is he?" her friend asked eagerly.

Together they pored over the leaflet. It read:

Evangelist MICHAEL RAINTREE
Preaching the Word nightly at
the Downtown Mission.
Come and hear the Word.
Learn the Truth!
Share the Gospel!
Hear the Sonshine Singers!
Food for the Souls of the Hungry

At the bottom was the address of the Mission and its hours.

"Ugh!" Monica said, wrinkling her nose. "What a seedy address."

"'Michael Raintree.'" Laura rolled the syllables around on her tongue, savoring them like candy. "I like that name."

"I like that *man!*" Monica sighed. "How can anybody be that good-looking and be . . ." she paused, searching for the right word, " . . . holy."

Laura gave her a half-smile. "I don't know. But I'd sure like to find out."

"What?" Monica asked. "You can't seriously be thinking of going down there?"

"Why not? I want to hear 'more,'" she said, quoting the leaflet.

"Your father will never allow it!"

"What he doesn't know . . ." Laura paused significantly. "Why don't you come with me?"

Monica threw back her head. "Not a chance! He's

17

absolutely gorgeous, but not worth the risk of being attacked."

"Don't be a bore," Laura chided. "I'm sure there's some kind of security . . ." She paused and glanced over the crowd that was now dispersing. He was gone. She stepped forward and scanned the waning afternoon shadows, but he was nowhere to be seen. And suddenly, she knew that she wanted to see him again. No matter what it took. No matter where she had to go to find him.

"But what about Fran's party?" Monica asked. "And Brad?"

"Not tonight," Laura said firmly and started back toward her parked car. "Fran and Brad will always be around. This Michael Raintree—whoever he is—may be gone after tonight."

Monica kept up a steady stream of "should nots" all the way to the car. Laura nodded but ignored her. She'd made up her mind. She wanted to see Michael Raintree once more. She didn't understand why, but she knew it was important. There was something about him. Something beyond his rugged good looks. Something burning in his eyes, his voice, his heart. A living fire. And she had to touch it one more time.

Laura was nervous, apprehensive, a little frightened as she entered the crowded, fluorescent-lit room of the Downtown Mission. Metal chairs, set up row by row, faced to the front of the room, where a card table and a shop-worn podium stood. The faint odor of cafeteria food and pine cleaner clung to the pale green walls.

She kept to the back of the room, chose a chair on an outside aisle and clutched her purse in her lap. In the back, near the door, she felt more at ease. If necessary, she could exit quickly without causing a disturbance. "Monica was right," she muttered to herself. "This was a stupid thing to do!"

18

She'd told herself the same thing all evening as she dressed, as she left the protective walls of her sprawling island estate, as she drove across the Rickenbacker Causeway and pulled into a parking space near the storefront. The bright mercury vapor lamps situated at regular intervals only advertised the danger and high crime reputation of the area.

But she was here now. And she was determined to see Michael Raintree again. Determined to know why the events of the afternoon had shaken her so profoundly. Determined to discover how this man, this evangelist with the violet-blue eyes, could touch her heart and her soul so powerfully.

Laura looked around the room curiously. Again, as in the afternoon, the people who had come to hear were the rejects of humanity, yet all of them were waiting expectantly. Like she was. She wondered why Michael had chosen to address this segment of society. Surely, with his charisma, he could be prominent in any church in the country.

She turned her attention to the singing group. They *did* make beautiful music, Laura conceded grudgingly. Though very different from the kind of music she was used to hearing in her own church, the simple songs spoke eloquently of the love of God. And the female singers' voices blended harmoniously.

One of them, a small-boned woman with long silky hair, had a particularly electrifying voice. Laura watched her intently. Her voice was powerful, yet lilting, with a haunting quality that lingered in one's ear. She was very pretty, too, Laura decided. Shimmering blond hair hung down her back to her waist, like a silver veil. Her features were small, dainty, feminine—in a fawnlike way. The expression on her face as she sang was one of rapture. *A man could love a woman who looked like that,* Laura thought ruefully. Then her heart gave a lurch. Maybe Michael Raintree loved her . . .

The singers finished their song. Voices from the crowd called out, "Praise the Lord!" and "Amen." Finally, another man, whom Laura recognized as the leaflet-bearer from the park, stepped up to the podium.

"As you know, I'm Billy Powell. I want to welcome all of you here tonight. After Michael finishes his message, you're all invited to stay around for ministry and fellowship. There are several of us who will be available to pray with you . . ." he paused, "and a kitchen full of doughnuts and coffee for you really 'hungry souls'!"

The people laughed aloud. Laura liked Billy Powell immediately. He had a soft Southern drawl and a down-home quality that spilled out of him as he spoke. His broad, ready smile was infectious.

"Well, I guess that's enough from me," Billy said. "I give you the man you have been waiting to hear— Michael Raintree."

Laura craned her neck. From where she was sitting, she couldn't even see the front row. As Michael strode to the podium, a hush fell over the room. Laura caught her breath. He was even more handsome than she remembered. His black hair held a hint of wave, and a stray lock trailed over his forehead.

He thrust his hands into the pockets of his navy blue slacks. A pale blue shirt, open at the neck, accentuated his broad shoulders. His jaw was firm, his eyebrows dark and thick. And although she couldn't see them, she knew firsthand about the devastating quality of his eyes.

Michael Raintree was a contradiction in terms, to Laura's way of thinking. His surroundings, the Mission, his listeners were the embodiment of poverty. But Michael the man—as evidenced by his clothes, his mannerisms, his educated speech, his style—was obviously from another world. A man who could command his own destiny. A man who could be equally at ease with beggars or boardroom chairmen. *I wonder what my father would think of you, Michael Raintree?* she asked silently. In some ways, they seemed to have been cut from the same cloth. Powerful, authoritative—born leaders of men.

"I want to tell you about a Man I know," Michael began. His voice sent shivers up her spine. A renewed hush fell over the room.

"Not unlike many of you, He was born in poverty—yet He grew up to revolutionize the world. He never fought a war. He never held a political office. He only had one message—the love of God for mankind. . . ." Slowly, Michael's words painted a portrait. A portrait of a Man both tender and fiery, both divine and human. A portrait of Jesus Christ.

As the verbal image emerged, Laura realized that she'd never seen this Christ before. She'd gone to church all her life. In fact, her family was one of the founding forces in the great stained-glass fortress she attended on an occasional Sunday. But she'd never encountered this victorious, life-changing Christ there. The image disquieted her. It disturbed her safe, preconceived notions about God.

Laura sat, riveted to her chair, Michael's words flowing over her. His voice held her like a magnet. His message erupted inside her soul and seared her heart. Part of her wanted to get up and run from the room. Another part wanted him to go on forever. It didn't seem possible that she could have lived all her life and never seen the Lord like this man had.

He talked for an hour. It seemed like only minutes. When he was finished the singing group came forward again. Their song was bold, triumphant. The blond woman's voice soared with hope and promise. And when it was over, the crowd rose to its feet, applauding. There was a surge of people around Michael. Laura longed to go to him, too. But she felt nervous, confused.

*Why should I feel like this?* she asked herself hotly. *He's only a preacher!* But she stood, transfixed, unable to make a move. Her thoughts tumbled and churned. His words had disturbed her. *He* disturbed her! *Why didn't I listen to Monica?* she berated herself for the hundredth time that night. *If only I'd gone to Fran's party. If only I'd spent the evening with Brad . . .*

But her self-incrimination was purposeless. She *had* come to see Michael. She *had* heard his message. And suddenly, she had to get out of there! She had to get home. Back to her safe insulated world, where there was no poverty, no confusing thoughts—no Michael Raintree.

One last time Laura searched the crowd for him. He looked up. Without warning, his eyes fixed on hers. The room, the people, the noise faded away. There was only Michael. Only this moment. Suspended in time, caught between today and tomorrow. His blue eyes penetrated her mind, her heart, her being. She began to tremble.

Then, without knowing why, she turned and fled into the night.

## CHAPTER 2

LAURA SAT at the enormous conference table, struggling to concentrate on the negotiations. The contract talks seemed to be taking forever. Her head ached. *Small wonder,* she thought, pressing her temples with her fingers. She hadn't slept much the night before. She'd lain in her bed and tossed and turned and watched the hands of her bedside clock tick off the hours of the long, lonely night.

And she thought of Michael Raintree. How could one human being have had such a devastating effect on her life? Only twenty-four hours before, she hadn't even known that he existed. And now . . . now he haunted her. Michael and . . . God.

"Don't you think so, Laura?"

She looked up guiltily from the yellow pad she'd been doodling on and focused on her father's face. She hadn't the vaguest notion what he was talking about.

"Sorry, Mac," she said. "I was thinking of something else." In the office she always called her father by his first name . When she'd first started working for him, there had been talk of nepotism among the other employees. But she'd worked hard. Mac had granted her no special favors. She'd earned her position in Garland Enterprises.

Mackenzie Garland shot her a warning look and then turned to the client with a counteroffer, "One and a half million, with 3 percent down, is the highest Goldstein will go, Mr. Mendez," he said.

Laura sighed. She usually enjoyed contract talks. She'd always found them stimulating. *Why can't I get with it this morning?* she thought. Her head throbbed and she rubbed her temples. She had been up by six AM after only a few fitful hours of sleep, had exercised vigorously in the gym room at her house, then had stood under the hot shower in the marbled private bath adjoining her bedroom suite. Somewhat refreshed, she had dressed carefully, choosing an emerald green silk shirtwaist that matched the color of her eyes. She had hoped the bright color would revive her. It hadn't.

She shook her mane of thick hair and wished she'd worn it up. The conference room seemed stuffy and close. Finally an agreement was reached between Mac on behalf of his client, and Mendez and his lawyer rose to leave. The lawyer, a bespectacled man with thinning hair, squeezed her hand a little too warmly as they left and whispered, "I'd like to take you to lunch today."

She looked at him with disdain and said, "I have a luncheon engagement."

His disappointment was obvious. "Perhaps another time?"

"I don't think so," she said gently. It was foolish to lead him on. She'd never go out with him.

"What's your problem?" Mac asked after the clients had left and he was alone with his daughter in the mahogany-paneled room. "For crying out loud, Laura," he fumed, "this was a two-million-dollar deal! You brought it in and then you all but checked out on it today!''

"I'm sorry, Mac," she sighed, leaning back in the plush leather chair. "I have a splitting headache . . ."

She looked at her father and forced a smile. Mac came and stood next to her, his hand resting tenderly on her shoulder. For all his gruffness she knew he hadn't really meant it. Laura was the light of his life. She always had been.

And Laura adored her father. He was a massively built man. Six feet tall and two hundred pounds, well-muscled, firm. At fifty-eight, he had the body and constitution of a much younger man. Then, he had earned it. He took excellent care of himself. Exercised daily. Played racketball three times a week, and still ran his business with dedication and integrity.

Mackenzie Garland had started his own construction company with Ted Jerrel on borrowed money soon after the end of World War II. The new enterprise demonstrated his faith in the growing Miami land market. "People will pay plenty to retire in the sun," he'd often said. So in the midfifties he'd taken outrageously daring risks on large parcels of raw, undeveloped land. The most notable was an island in Biscayne Bay, where he'd built a bridge and constructed hundred-thousand-dollar homes.

"Garland's crazy!" his detractors had said. "Who'd pay that much to live on an island?"

As it turned out, plenty of people. Gull Island was still one of the most prestigious addresses in the city. Mac's own home, a sprawling Palm-Beach-style mansion, was built on the choicest lot. Laura loved that house. She still lived there, comfortable in her relationship with her parents, secure in the plush surroundings of her luxurious lifestyle.

Her father's construction firm was worth millions when he sold it and moved exclusively into real estate in the late sixties, with holdings throughout Florida,

25

Nassau, and even South America. Laura often marveled at his ability to manage such diverse holdings and still be involved with his only daughter's day-to-day life.

"You went out alone last night, came home late, and disappeared into your room," Mac said.

Laura bristled. One of her conditions for remaining at home when her other unmarried friends had long since moved into their own apartments was complete freedom to come and go as she pleased, no questions asked. She'd taken the responsibility seriously. She admired her parents. She'd never do anything to disgrace them or her family name. "Now, now!" Mac cautioned. "Don't get your back up. I'm not checking on you. I'm just worried about you."

She smiled and stood to kiss his forehead. "Thanks," she said, but ignored his probe into her private life. "I told Monica I'd meet her for lunch. Do you mind if I take off?"

"Take the rest of the day," he urged. "You're no good to me moping around here."

"Thanks," she called and headed for the door. For some reason she felt as if she'd been let out of prison. She picked up her yellow pad and glanced at it as she headed for the elevators. One word was scribbled across the top: *Michael*. She didn't even remember writing it! She tore off the page angrily and wadded it into a tight ball.

Outside, the warm January sun beat down on her head and shoulders. The cold snap had ended. The mercury was already well into the seventies. Laura slid behind the wheel of her red Thunderbird and slipped into the flow of noonday traffic. The '57 vintage convertible had been a gift from her parents on her twenty-third birthday. "They don't make them like this anymore!" Mac had boomed when he handed her the keys. He was right. She had enjoyed the car

26

immensely and still received admiring glances as she zipped around town.

She parked behind the restaurant in Coral Gables, went inside, and was immediately seated. Naturally, Monica was late. Laura felt irritated. Monica was never on time! She scanned the gourmet menu while a waiter hovered nearby. She disliked the place anyway. It was overdone and pretentious. But Monica loved it and so they met there often.

"Sorry, luv . . ." Monica said breathlessly as she glided up to the table. "Been waiting long?"

"What was it today?" Laura asked crossly.

"Raul couldn't get the color right," Monica explained. "I thought I'd never get out of there." Even in the dim lighting of the restaurant, Laura could see that Monica's blond pageboy was several shades lighter. "I wanted it more silvery this time," she explained.

With a pang, her words brought up the memory of the delicate and lovely singer Laura had seen last night at the Mission. It would have been cruel to tell Monica that some people were born with hair that color.

"So tell me *all* about last night," Monica begged. "I thought about you all during Fran's party. You were right—it was a bore. Hope you got close to that gorgeous preacher! How did it go? Tell me!"

Monica's attitude annoyed Laura. What happened last night was not some juicy tidbit of gossip to be bantered about over lunch. It had been a moving and emotional experience. She determined to say nothing more than was necessary. "He's a wonderful preacher," she said in a noncommittal tone.

"Oh, come now!" Monica drawled.

Fortunately, she was interrupted by the arrival of a waiter. He bowed slightly and held out a silver tray. On it lay a single red rose. "From the gentleman at the far table," he explained.

27

Both women turned to look in the direction of the handsome blond man in an immaculate blue suit, who raised his wine glass in a silent tribute to Laura. "It's Brad Meyers!" Monica whispered. "Oh, Laura, he's coming over here."

Laura smiled slightly as Brad approached.

"Thank you," she said softly, lifting the rose to inhale the sweet fragrance. "It's lovely."

"So are you," Brad said, a look of open admiration in his gray-green eyes. "I'm right in the middle of a business luncheon, but when I saw you walk in, I couldn't resist," he told her. "Missed you at the party last night."

Laura shrugged. "There'll be other parties."

Brad leaned closer. The smell of his cologne was heady and masculine. Laura felt a warm color creep into her cheeks. She was glad it was dark in the restaurant. "Could I take you to dinner tonight?" he asked, his voice was warm, suggestive.

"Tonight?" she asked. It was tempting. Then a memory pressed unbidden into her thoughts—the memory of Michael Raintree. His words, his voice, his mission. And she knew she couldn't go out with Brad that night. Not until she settled some questions in her own mind about the things she'd heard and felt.

"I-I can't tonight, Brad . . ." she said, genuinely sorry. "But please ask again."

He took her hand and squeezed it warmly. "It's a deal," he said, a half-smile turning up the corners of his sensuous mouth. "I'll call you," he promised, then left their table.

"What could you possibly have to do that is more important than a date with Brad Meyers?" Monica asked in disbelief.

Laura buried her face in her menu, hoping to ignore the question.

But Monica wouldn't be put off. "You're going

28

back to that scuzzy little Mission?" she barked accusingly.

Laura dropped her menu with defiance, "What if I am?" A look of earnestness crossed her lovely features. "Please, try to understand, Monica. Michael Raintree isn't like anyone I've ever met in my whole life. I *must* know more about him." She paused, struggled for a moment, then added, "And about God."

Monica narrowed her eyes and scrutinized Laura's face. "You're perfectly serious, aren't you?"

Laura nodded.

Monica took a deep breath and said, "All right. Go find out what you have to. But be careful."

Laura was grateful that her friend hadn't tried to argue with her. She picked up the rose and pressed it to her cheek. The subtle fragrance filled her senses. She closed her eyes, trying to call up Brad's tanned good looks. But all she saw were the soul-searing eyes of Michael Raintree.

Laura drove down the winding back road with almost reckless abandon. Huge oaks spread a leafy canopy over the road, casting sun-flecked shadows across her car. The wind whipped her hair and swirled it about her face. Driving at breakneck speed, seemingly one with the machine, Laura could think more clearly. The rushing wind cleared her mind of cobwebs and blew fresh purpose into her thoughts.

Why had she turned down Brad's dinner invitation? What was wrong with her anyway? He was a very attractive man and she felt a strong physical attraction for him. Yet, she'd refused a date with him. And for what? To sit in some poverty-stricken Mission in a world populated by the poor, the elderly, the hopeless?

*Maybe that's it*, she thought. *Maybe that's what Michael dispenses . . . hope.* She'd felt purposeless before, and in need of hope. But hope for what? Was Monica right? Was she throwing away the opportunity to be loved? To be *in* love? "Fool!" she said aloud, the wind flinging her word into the afternoon air.

She slowed for a curve, geared down, then hit the accelerator. The car strained forward. A half-smile crossed her face. "You know what your problem is, Laura? You've never been in love." Not really. Oh, she'd played the game many times. But love—real, deep, abiding love—had always eluded her

What would Monica think if she knew that no man had ever made love to her, Laura wondered. Not that she hadn't been tempted. Yet, giving herself to a man, body and soul, had seemed too precious a commitment to be taken as lightly as Monica and her other friends took it.

At times in her life, Laura's virginity had seemed a burden to her. An old-fashioned thing to be discarded. But she never had. Because it was a part of herself worth saving, to be given out of love—to one special man. One day she would give herself totally. But to whom?

Her dream lover never had a face. In her romantic fantasies, he used to appear and sweep her off into the sunset. But she was too old for fairy tales now. Too wise for romantic illusions.

Laura took a deep breath, glancing at her gold Piaget wristwatch. She slowed her car, turned off the two-lane road and cut over to the traffic-glutted Causeway that would take her home. It was getting late. She'd have just enough time to shower and change before the evening service at the Mission.

A look of determination settled on her pretty face. Tonight she wouldn't run away. Tonight she'd face the stranger who caused her feelings to churn so wildly within her. Tonight she'd conquer the demons that pricked her mind over Michael Raintree—once and for all!

The Mission was crowded. Laura tried to slip in, unnoticed. But several people turned their heads and stared as she came inside. She kept her eyes downcast, avoiding visual contact with anyone.

The back rows were already filled. She carefully threaded her way to one lone chair on the aisle. It was much too close to the front. She'd have preferred to be farther back, but she had no other choice. The crowd sat patiently—some reading Bibles; others talking softly among themselves. Already she recognized faces from the previous night.

When the Sonshine Singers played their melodies, every person in the place listened attentively, many humming and mouthing the words. Laura first searched the backs of the heads in the first row for Michael. She found him, stared momentarily, then turned her attention to the singers.

The blond woman's voice was as enchanting as ever. *So is she,* Laura admitted to herself, watching the lithe swaying figure of the petite beauty. After three or four more praise songs, Billy Powell rose and walked to the front of the group.

"Don't they sing pretty?" Billy asked, open admiration in his eyes. The audience agreed. "Let me introduce them to you," Billy said. "At the keyboard is Jack Mora. The brunette songbird is his sister Lisa. Our guitarist is Phil Chandler. And the lady with the voice of an angel is Chris Avery."

*Chris . . .* Laura thought. The face had a name. *Chris . . .* As the applause died away, Michael stood and walked to the front of the room. Laura felt herself tense. Her stomach constricted and she licked her lips nervously. His presence shouldn't affect her like that, she thought. Yet, it did.

He scanned the faces of his listeners. She dropped her eyes. She didn't want to meet his gaze again.

"How many of you have found purpose for your lives?" Michael asked. "How many of you know

31

what you're supposed to be doing with your time—
your days . . . your hours?"

Laura's breath caught in her throat. Why would he
ask that question? How could Michael possibly know
what was going on inside her?

He continued, "Have you been living from day to
day, yet have no contentment? No sense of peace?"

It was impossible! As he talked, Laura felt that he
was revealing her most intimate thoughts—as if he'd
found her diary and was reading it aloud to all these
strangers! She listened, not daring to move, for fear
everyone in the room would turn and stare at her.
Then everyone would know that Michael was talking
about her . . . Laura Garland. There was no escape.
She could only sit and listen, mesmerized by his
presence.

"As human beings," Michael said, "we have but
one purpose under the sun, one goal—and that is to
glorify God. We have a biblical mandate to take
dominion over the earth, to make disciples of all
nations, to glorify God . . ."

As his voice filled the room, Laura felt the strength
of his commitment. His words filled her with wonder.
The impact of his message pressed against her,
stirring something deep within—something so myste-
rious, so curious, that she could not give it a name.
The things Michael had said, the Christ he had shown
her, inflamed her imagination, incited her mind, and
left her with a growing hunger for more.

The answers were so simple; the message, so clear;
the truth, so plain. Somehow she, too, was meant to
glorify God. The door to her entire future was
standing before her. And Michael Raintree held the
key. It seemed obvious as he spoke. After tonight's
meeting was over, she would go up and meet him.
And tell him. And he would help her. He *had* to!

However, when the meeting finally broke up, Laura
sat unmoving in her chair while people milled about

her. She could see Michael at the front of the room, surrounded by eager people. But she couldn't bring herself to get up, walk forward, and approach him.

Suddenly, she felt a touch on her shoulder. "Oh!" she gasped, jumping up.

"I'm sorry. I didn't mean to startle you."

Laura caught her breath and turned to look into the face of Lisa, the pert pixyish brunette singer from the Sonshine Singers. Masses of thick brown curls framed a heart-shaped face. Her eyes were hazel, bright and sparkling. They crinkled at the corners when she smiled. A smattering of light brown freckles dusted her turned-up nose. Laura liked her instantly, sensing a deep joy and serenity coming from within Lisa's character.

"I-It's all right," Laura stammered.

"I've noticed you the past couple of nights," Lisa smiled warmly. "I was wondering if I might answer any questions for you."

Laura answered a bit too quickly, "No . . . really. I was just listening . . ." Laura picked up her purse and prepared to leave.

"Would you like to meet Michael?" Lisa asked.

"Oh, I don't think so . . ." Laura said.

But Lisa took her by her arm and pulled her toward the front of the room. "I'm Lisa Mora," she said. "And you are . . . ?"

"Laura . . ." Laura said uneasily, as they drew closer to Michael.

When Lisa reached out and touched his arm, he turned, fastening his cobalt-blue eyes onto Laura's face. "This is Laura," Lisa began.

". . . Garland," Laura finished weakly. "I-I heard you in the park the other day . . ." She felt like a butterfly pinned under glass.

"Red." Michael said cryptically.

"I-I beg your pardon?" Laura stammered, caught off guard by his response.

"You were wearing red," he said simply. "A red jacket. A red dress."

Now she was totally flustered. She didn't know what to say. A warm blush began to creep up her neck and into her cheeks. She felt like bolting for the door. He had remembered her! What could he possibly think of her? That she was some moon-struck groupie? "I-I came to hear you preach again . . ." she said, a bit defensively.

He regarded her from head to toe, as if appraising her. His voice was cool as he told her, "My message is for everyone, Miss Garland. But for your own good, for your own safety, may I suggest that you don't show up down here in two-hundred-dollar silk dresses and hundred-dollar shoes. Not all of my 'congregation' are God-fearing, hard-working, self-sufficient citizens."

Laura only stood and stared at him. Then slowly, hot tears of humiliation sprang to her eyes. She quickly backed away, clutching her leather handbag to herself. Then for the second time in as many nights, Laura turned and hurried off into the night.

# CHAPTER 3

"YOU CERTAINLY SEEM DISTRACTED this morning, Laura," Ellen Garland said. Laura didn't miss the edge of annoyance in her mother's voice. "I thought that when you didn't go in to the office this morning, we might enjoy a nice leisurely breakfast together. You've hardly touched anything."

Laura leaned back in the comfortable patio chair at the glass-topped breakfast table and pushed away her plate of crepes with strawberry sauce. "Not hungry," she said.

She looked out over the tranquil turquoise waters of the swimming pool. The water was so calm . . . so different from the emotions that roiled inside her. Last night had been a disaster! Instead of talking to Michael, she had run away. Her cheeks still burned with the memory of his chastisement.

"Well, if you're not going to eat, then please don't sit there sulking," Ellen said crossly. "We see too little of each other for you to waste our time together by pouting."

*Pouting* . . . Laura thought. To Ellen, Laura was

still a child. She observed her mother's face. At fifty-five, Ellen was still lovely. Her perfectly coiffured dark brown hair was streaked with strands of gray—which she'd steadfastly refused to color away. "I earned every one of these gray hairs," she'd often remarked. Ellen's eyes were pale green, and partially shielded by fashionable half-glasses that perched on her thin high-bridged nose.

She wore a flowing silk chiffon dressing gown of a palest peach color. An enormous diamond ring sparkling from her left hand represented thirty-one years of marriage to Mackenzie Garland. Laura often wondered if they had been happy years.

Growing up on the sumptuous island estate had been lonely for Laura as an only child. Her parents had been very busy people—Mac, with his business; Ellen, with her club and social work. It was what was expected of them. Her parents had seemed contented, but distant, both involved in their own worlds.

For their sakes and ever aware of their position in the community, Laura had been a "good" girl, never causing her parents worry or shame. Oh, she and Monica had done some pretty reckless and crazy things while growing up, but in retrospect their antics had been pretty tame.

Now, as she sat on the poolside patio of her home, surveying her mother, Laura wondered again where her own life was headed. Marriage? Permanent career? A social life filled with charities, bazaars, and parties? She shuddered at *that* thought. She had never been overly fond of the social scene. Most parties only bored her.

"I have a committee meeting at ten this morning," Ellen reported. "For the Diabetes Center. You know their annual fund-raising dinner-dance is coming up next month."

"Fine, Mother," Laura said, peremptorily, then abruptly stood to discourage further conversation.

"I'm going for a quick swim." She dropped her cover-up onto a chair, revealing her long-legged, perfectly proportioned body. She filled out the sleek lavender swimsuit impressively.

"Is the water warm enough?"

"The pool heater's been on since November, Mother," Laura reminded her. Then she balanced gracefully on the tiled side of the pool and plunged headfirst into the inviting aqua waters. The water felt fresh and invigorating. She stayed beneath the surface, allowing the water to block out all the sounds of the morning. Then she split the surface and quickly swam ten laps.

When she finished, Laura exited the pool, and kissed Ellen lightly on her cheek. "I need to dress."

"But we've hardly spent any time together," Ellen complained. "You left last night without even telling Miranda you had other dinner plans. Besides, your father and I missed you terribly at dinner . . ."

"Miranda is just a mother-hen," Laura fussed, remembering their plump cook, who'd been with them since the Cuban crisis of the early sixties. "I had someplace to go last night."

"What about tonight?" Ellen called after her as Laura opened the patio French doors and started into the house.

"No plans . . ." she said grimly, determined to stay away from Michael and his Mission.

In her room, Laura stepped out onto her private balcony that overlooked the bay. The sun bounced brilliantly off the bright green water. "What *am* I going to do today?" she wondered aloud. The day was so lovely. And she felt so restless. Like a caged animal.

She heard a soft knock on her bedroom door. "Yes?"

"Telephone for you, Miss Laura," the housemaid, Inez, said.

*Now what?* she thought crossly. She couldn't bear to think of another purposeless day, flitting about department stores and boutiques with Monica. "I'll take it up here, Inez. Thank you." Laura crossed the thick white carpet of her room to her antique desk and picked up the receiver of her phone. "Hello," she said.

"Miss Garland?" a deep male voice asked.

Her heart began to pound uncontrollably. His voice was unmistakable.

"This is Michael Raintree," he began. His introduction was extraneous.

"Yes," she said, afraid her voice might begin to shake as much as her hands, now gripping the receiver convulsively.

"I believe I owe you an apology."

"It-it's not necessary . . ."

"Lisa told me I acted like a clod," he said firmly. "She was right. I was rude and insensitive. I'm sorry."

"You don't owe me anything, Mr. Raintree," Laura said, her heart thumping wildly.

"I owe you more than an apology. If you have no other plans, would you have lunch with me?"

"I-I'd like that very much."

"Good!" his voice boomed with enthusiasm. "How about noon?"

"That would be fine." Suddenly, she grew self-conscious. She didn't want him to come to her house, running the risk that her wealth and opulence might affront him. "Why don't I come to the Mission?" she offered cheerfully. "It would be easier than trying to direct you here."

"Something tells me you don't live on the bus line . . ."

She laughed aloud. "I'll be there at noon," she said, her spirits soaring.

"I thought we could go on a picnic. It's such a

38

beautiful day. Warm, too. I'll bring all the making for a perfect picnic, Miss Garland."

"Please," she urged, "call me Laura."

"See you soon, Laura," Michael's voice was suddenly softer.

She hung up and let out a shout, dancing across the room. "I'm going out with Michael!" she told her reflection in the bathroom mirror. She decided against a quick shower, and, instead, turned on the gold swan-necked spigots of her sunken marble tub, filled it with rose-scented water and took a leisurely bath, dreaming of the hours ahead.

She tried on five outfits before settling on the right one. Odd, she'd never noticed before that her wardrobe leaned to silk dresses and silk blouses. With a dressing room full of clothes, there was nothing suitable to wear on a date with Michael. She finally chose a jewel green silk shirt and designer jeans, tossed a camel suede jacket over her shoulders and surveyed the results in her dressing room mirror.

Her eyes looked very green, slightly slanted over high delicate cheekbones, and honey-colored hair curled full and scented to her shoulders. Flushed cheeks gave her an expectant and radiant look, subtly enhanced with make-up to magnify her natural beauty. "Hope you like it, too, Michael," she whispered to her reflection.

Hurriedly, she left her room, her heart singing.


Laura pulled up in front of the Mission. The warm sun beat down, bouncing off the sidewalk. When the front door of the Mission opened, Michael emerged, carrying a basket in one hand and a blanket in the other.

"Hi," he smiled broadly. "You're right on time."

She blushed, hoping her punctuality wouldn't make her appear overly eager. "Just shove the goodies behind the seat, in the rear space," she directed. A

39

thought came to her. "Would you like to drive?" she asked.

He grinned. "Yes." She got out and walked around as he held open the door. Then he took his place behind the wheel, curling up his long legs and grasping the steering wheel with purpose. "Hang on!" he directed and slipped effortlessly into the sparse traffic.

Conversation was impossible as they drove, so Laura watched him from the corner of her eye. The car became a slave to him, a willing servant that purred and hummed and sang with every gear shift, every acceleration. The wind whipped his black hair and she saw the pulsebeat in his temple.

He was such an enigma. His clothes, his self-assurance, his voice, indicated that he was well educated. Certainly he was well spoken. Yet beneath his surface there simmered a passion for life, a dedication to principle, a love and a zest for living, a driving Force. He was a man in complete control, unworried by life's everyday hassles, undisturbed by a world that bowed to materialism and self-indulgence. And he fascinated her totally.

As he drove along the boulevard, she watched the blue waters of the bay sparkle in the noonday sun, its surface flecked with sailboats out to capture the balmy breezes. The sky stretched overhead like a blue canvas, dappled with puffy white clouds.

Michael's destination was North Miami. He followed a curving road and turned into the entrance of Greynolds Park. "Ever been here?" he asked as he parked the sports car.

"Never," she told him. She'd lived in Miami all her life and had probably never seen half of it. Why not? Because people of her social class didn't mingle with most of the inhabitants of the city, she realized. She felt slightly ashamed of that and hoped Michael wouldn't find her out.

"Come on," he directed. He picked up the picnic

40

items and she followed along beside him. The park stretched in front of them, a sun-spangled luscious confectionery dipped in vats of green and brown and gray. Leaves fluttered and rustled. Streamers of moss floated in the faint breeze. The subtle perfumes of bougainvillaea and wild orchids hung in the air. Michael brought her to the foot of a hill in the center of the park.

"A hill in Miami?" she giggled.

"Up there," he pointed. "It's a lookout tower constructed out of solid coral rock." High atop the hill was a fortresslike circular structure. "We'll climb up later and look around. You can see a long way off," he told her. He spread the blanket on the grass at the base of the hill and invited Laura to sit with him. Then he spread out a luscious collection of goodies. "Made this with my own two hands," he said.

Her mouth fairly watered. She remembered that she'd eaten no breakfast. Now she was ravenous. He'd brought fresh, chewy bagels, smoked salmon, cream cheese, clusters of green grapes and tart tangy apples. He poured them each a glass of sparkling water. The bubbles tickled her nose as she drank it.

"Some lunch!" Laura teased. "Whipped it up yourself, huh?"

"I confess," Michael laughed. "There's a delicatessen three blocks from the Mission. Mrs. Bergman whipped it up."

"My regards to Mrs. Bergman." Laura said. It felt so good and natural to be sitting across from Michael. His presence still overwhelmed her somewhat, but she was beginning to feel more at ease in his company.

A blue jay hopped boldly to the corner of their blanket. Michael tossed him some bread crumbs. Laura watched the man. There was so much she wanted to know. So much she wanted to hear. "Who

41

are you, Michael?'' she asked softly. "Where do you come from? How did you become an evangelist?''

He turned the full attention of his marvelous blue eyes on her and drew a deep breath before answering her question. ''I didn't start out very religious. In fact, back home in West Virginia, I was a constant source of grief to my family, I'm afraid. My folks have a small farm near a town that's too small to be on most maps.

"When I was growing up, I was in and out of so much trouble that I thought my dad was going to disown me. My grandma lived with us. She was a very religious woman. Prayed for me daily, or I'd probably have been dead before my twentieth birthday.'' A small smile played on his mouth and he tossed a single blade of grass into the sky.

"My dad drove a truck on an interstate delivery route to help make ends meet. He got so he took me on trips with him. It was easier than getting me out of scrapes when he came home from the road.''

Laura listened, fascinated. She tried to imagine Michael in constant trouble. She bet most of it had centered around girls.

A squirrel scampered to the side of the blanket, stood on his haunches, and sniffed the air. "On one trip, we were hurrying to get home before Christmas.'' Michael's words transported her from the green warmth of the park to the chilling cold of a long-ago winter. "We were traveling through the mountains. It was bitterly cold. Ice on the roads. Dad lost control of his truck. It went over the embankment.''

Laura instinctively recoiled, imagining Michael crushed beneath the wheels. He continued, ''My dad was thrown from the truck. He died instantly. I, on the other hand, didn't have a scratch on me. I lay pinned in that truck for three hours before the Highway Patrol found me.

"When I got home, and after Dad's funeral,

Grandma came up to me. She leveled her blue eyes straight into mine and said, 'Michael, I reckon the Good Lord has put out His hand and saved ya. Can't say why. But, if I was you, boy, I'd git myself into church, git down on my knees and ask Him!' "

"And that's exactly what I did." Michael paused. The squirrel ventured timidly forward as Michael offered the gray ball of fuzz a morsel of bagel. "The answer didn't come all at once. I wasn't even saved then. But one day I knew that I was meant to preach the gospel—to the poor, the lost, the lonely; people who had no hope, no reason to go on with their lives."

The squirrel took the handout, retreated to the safety of a tree and ate greedily. "You don't seem like a farm boy . . ." Laura ventured, unable to suppress her curiosity.

His eyes sparkled, amused, and she felt a spreading warmth travel up her neck and throat and across her cheeks. "I traveled to *plenty* of rural churches, preaching. My own church helped raise enough money to send me to seminary—a small school, fundamental, nondenominational. Believe it or not, I really took to the books. Turned into quite a scholar. Spent two years studying at Oxford in England . . . preaching wherever I could. I toured Europe. Went to the ancient cathedrals. Walked where Luther, Calvin, Wesley walked . . . kind of immersed myself in tradition and church heritage."

In her mind's eye she saw Michael, touring Europe, igniting theological fires in staid, proper halls of learning, and in the majestic old churches of the past.

"When I came back home," he continued, I knew that I had to go on taking the Word of God to the people. I became a guest lecturer, evangelist, preacher. In Texas, Billy Powell hooked up with me. He's been my right arm ever since.

"In California, I found the Sonshine Singers . . ."

At the mention of the singers, Laura leaned forward. She didn't want to miss anything he had to say about the beautiful Chris Avery. "They also felt led to become a part of my ministry. That was three years ago. We've been together ever since."

"Why are you in Miami?"

"A minister friend invited me. He wanted me to set up the Downtown Mission. So many poor and old people are down there. Crime is rampant. The Mission is to be a kind of a haven for them. A place to go, hear God's Word, fellowship . . ." He took a sip of the sparkling water. "I've still got a lot of work to do there."

Laura watched the shadows of the afternoon begin to lengthen. The grassy hillside flowed to the edge of their blanket like thick green frosting. A few leaves danced over the remains of their picnic.

"Come on," Michael said, standing up and pulling Laura to her feet. "We need to stretch our legs."

She fell into step beside him, thoughtful, her mind still dwelling on his reminiscences. "Tell me about yourself," he said.

She shrugged. Her existence seemed colorless by comparison. She told about her parents, her father's real estate firm, her job. She talked quickly, hoping he wouldn't ask too many probing questions. It wasn't that she didn't want him to know. It was just that it all seemed so shallow somehow.

The two of them walked along the footpaths. Laura watched the sunlight dancing across his broad shoulders and black hair. Leaf patterns shaped by sunless shadows fell over his back. The late afternoon air filled her senses with the poignant promise of endless summer. She wished she could forever preserve the time and space they occupied . . . taking it out and reliving it in years to come.

"I have to get back," he said finally. "I preach again tonight." He turned and faced her. Laura's pulse raced. He took both her hands in his, holding her at arm's length and looked down on her from his towering height. She longed to have him pull her close to him, to feel the protective circle of his arms. For the briefest moment, she thought he would. But the moment passed. He squeezed her hands and tapped her on the tip of her nose. "Thank you for today." His voice sounded husky. "I needed to relax. You helped me forget how tired I am."

In those words she had the faintest glimmer into the complexity of his life. How demanding and soul-draining his call must be on him. She was very grateful that she could have served him in some small way. They gathered up their picnic items and walked to the car. They drove to the Mission in silence, Laura content with the physical nearness of him.

When he got out of the car, she looked up at him shyly. "I-I'd like to hear you preach again tonight," she ventured cautiously. "I promise to leave my expensive clothes at home . . ."

He threw back his head and laughed heartily. "I deserve that . . . Yes. Please come. I'll look for you." Then he gave her a brief salute and vanished inside the building.

On her way home, Laura made one stop. She went to the closest department store and bought two outfits. Each was tasteful and becoming. Yet, neither had designer labels or designer prices. When she arrived home, she went first to the library and searched the shelves until she found a short row of Bibles. Each Bible was bound in rich subtle leather, gilded along its edges. She thumbed through each one and, with a start, realized that they were all practically brand-new, even though some had been sitting on the shelf for years. They were, for the most part, completely unused.

Next, she told Miranda not to set a place for her at dinner. She left a quick note for her parents, explaining she had other plans for the evening. Finally, she went to her suite.

As she opened the door, the sweet heady smell of roses filled her nostrils. On her antique desk, Inez had placed a magnificent bouquet of velvety red roses. "How beautiful!" she cried aloud. She crossed the room and bent to inhale their lovely fragrance, then picked up a card attached to the vase. It read: "Dinner tomorrow night? Love, Brad."

A frown furrowed her forehead. Brad! She had all but forgotten about him. Why couldn't the roses have been from Michael?

"But how could they be?" she asked herself aloud.

Where would Michael get that kind of money? And for the first time it occurred to her that money meant absolutely nothing to a man like Michael. In honesty she was forced to ask herself, "What does it mean to me?"


Laura sat in the audience and listened with rapt attention to every word Michael uttered. She tried hard to look up the passages in her Bible as he referred to them, but she was a pitiful Bible scholar. She couldn't find most of the various books without first looking at the table of contents. Her ignorance angered her.

How was it that she had been going to church all her life and didn't even know the books of the Bible? How could she have been so near God, yet so far from Him at the same time? How could Michael Raintree have so totally revolutionized her life in three short days?

When the meeting ended, Laura felt a bit more comfortable hanging around, waiting for Michael to finish his conversations with the people who flocked around him. She watched. How exhausting it must be for him! All those people—anxious, hungry, longing for what he had to give. She was deep in thought, watching him intently, when she felt a nudge on her arm.

Laura spun around and found herself looking into the cool blue eyes of Chris Avery. The girl's manner was aloof and standoffish. "You've been coming here for the past three nights." The statement seemed an accusation, delivered with a chill in her voice. "Michael told me that you went on a picnic with him this afternoon. I just want you to be aware, Laura Garland," Chris said coldly, "many, many women have been attracted to Michael and have used his message as a pretense to get closer to him. It has never worked. Michael always sees through them to their real intentions. Always!" Then she turned on her heel and walked away, her stream of silver-gold hair flowing behind her.

## CHAPTER 4

LAURA STOOD, OPEN-MOUTHED, staring after Chris as she was swallowed up by the crowd of people in the Mission. She felt as if Chris had dealt her a blow to her stomach. As if she'd been slapped. The woman's words had been cruel; their intent, to wound.

Laura felt color creep into her face. Chris had meant to put her down . . . and she had succeeded. Once again, Laura had to face the reality of her confused emotions about Michael. She *was* attracted to the man. That was a fact. But she was also attracted to his message—drawn by the power of his personal relationship to God and his fiery representation of Christ as a personalized Savior.

"You okay?" The question startled Laura. She turned to find Lisa standing at her side, and she flushed even more deeply. Yet, Lisa's kind hazel eyes delivered an unspoken message of understanding and friendship.

"I'm fine . . ." Laura said softly.

"She doesn't mean it, you know." Lisa's gaze followed Chris. "She's very protective of Michael.

We all are," Lisa added hastily. "He pushes himself much too hard. He rarely takes a day off. Frankly, I'm glad the two of you were able to go off today for a picnic. It's the most relaxed I've seen him in weeks."

Laura nodded, noticing the throng of people pressed around the podium, trying to speak privately with Michael. There were so many. So many who were poor. So many who were old. So many—hungry for the spiritual food of his ministry.

"Why don't you come on into the kitchen and help me put out the coffee and doughnuts?" Lisa asked kindly.

Quickly Laura agreed. She followed Lisa into the decrepit kitchen, grateful for something to do. Something to keep her hands busy and to occupy her confused thoughts.

The kitchen, brightly lit by florescent lights that cast a spell of surrealism over the room, held a long work table, a chipped porcelain sink and equipment that was antiquated and worn; yet everything appeared spotlessly clean. As if reading her thoughts, Lisa said, "You should have seen this place when we first arrived. What a pig sty! Chris and I scrubbed the place on our hands and knees. I'll bet we removed six inches of dirt and grime."

"Why do you do it?" Laura asked cautiously.

"Are you kidding?" Lisa laughed, her eyes crinkling at the corners. "A person could catch a disease from some of these places!"

Laura realized that Lisa had misinterpreted her real question. "No," she said. "Why do you travel around with Michael? Your singing group could probably be at the top of the charts with the right manager. You're very good, you know."

Lisa paused in her work of arranging doughnuts on aluminum serving trays. "We believe in it," she told Laura, passing over Laura's praise of the group. "God has done so much for us. Given us not only

49

salvation, but real miracles in all our lives. It's such a little bit of time and energy to give back to Him. The Sonshine Singers have a long and rocky history— each of us individually, all of us as a group." She smiled to herself. Laura wanted to know more, but was reluctant to pry. Lisa continued over her shoulder as she resumed her work, "We believe in Michael's ministry. He's an evangelist called to serve the world. He spreads the gospel to people who would otherwise never hear it. Without men like Michael, how would they ever learn the truth?" she asked.

"He could preach in a regular church," Laura suggested.

"True. And believe me, many churches have asked him. But that's not really what he's called by God to do. A lot of denominations contribute financially to his work. They recognize him as a true modern-day apostle—a man who goes about preaching the Word and setting up new churches. And he does it very well," she mused. "Also . . ." she added, almost shyly, "I have a personal reason for staying around."

Laura tilted her head, ready to pursue the topic, when Billy Powell stuck his head through the doorway of the kitchen and drawled, "What's the hold-up? The natives are getting restless out here."

The look on Lisa's face as her eyes met Billy's answered Laura's unspoken question. The two of them were in love. For a moment, she felt like an intruder into their private world, but the moment passed when Billy took the doughnut-laden tray from Lisa and, with a wink, left the kitchen.

After the food was served, Laura wandered through the Mission feeling self-conscious, purposeless. Billy, the Sonshine Singers, Michael . . . they all had important things to do. People to talk with, pray with, listen to. She, on the other hand, had nothing. Laura longed to be nearer Michael, but he was still sur-

50

rounded. She wouldn't feel right if she distracted or interrupted him.

She also stayed clear of Chris, who politely ignored her. In the end, she gathered up her things, glanced wistfully back toward Michael and left the Mission, unnoticed.

She drove home in a pensive, almost melancholy mood. What was she to do now? Having known Michael, could she ever put him out of her mind? Could she continue with her life as if the past few days had never happened? As if he had never challenged her safe, sheltered world or her unrealistic notions about an abstract, uninvolved God? As if he'd never held up to her very soul the mirror of his violet-blue eyes?

Laura sat in her office, poring over the lengthy contract. It was tedious work, but necessary. As a realtor, she had to keep her client's interests foremost in her mind at all times. No matter how viable a contract might be, if it wasn't in her client's best interests, she couldn't present it.

Her phone buzzed on her desk. Absently, she reached for the receiver. "Yes?"

A deep male voice answered, "Laura?"

For a moment her heart skipped and she caught her breath. "It's Brad," the caller said.

She felt a fleeting bit of disappointment as she said,"Brad! How good to hear from you." Why couldn't it have been Michael? "Thank you so much for the roses."

"They came with an invitation to dinner," he reminded her. "How about it?"

She paused briefly, weighing her options. She felt she should stay away from the Mission for a few days. She needed some time and space between herself and the people there. Besides, it would be fun to go out for a good time with an attractive man. And Brad *was* attractive to her. Most attractive.

"I'd like that," she said.

"Good," he told her. "I'll pick you up about eight. I'll make reservations at the Chateau Parisienne on the Beach. After dinner, we can take in the show."

Once she hung up, Laura sat twirling her pencil. Perhaps a date with Brad would be the tonic she needed to lift herself from her doldrums. After all, they had been reared in similar worlds, with similar values and backgrounds. They traveled in the same social circles. They found each other mutually attractive.

She dressed carefully for the evening, choosing a Paris designer original of black silk, embossed with black embroidered butterflies. Her skin gleamed, burnished and golden. Her hair lay on her shoulders in sculptured waves, with wisps and tendrils near her cheeks. Brad's low whistle of appreciation when he picked her up reinforced what her mirror had already revealed to her. Laura Garland was beautiful. She absently wondered if Michael would have thought so, too. . . .

Brad was a gifted conversationalist. He told her of his work as a stock market investor, his hobby of sailing, his interest in jogging and racketball. She listened pleasantly during the ride to Miami Beach in his plush Mercedes.

Brad drove up and around the vast circular driveway of the famous beach hotel noted for its gourmet French restaurant. A solicitous valet opened Laura's car door, then drove off to park the car. Brad and Laura ascended the broad red-carpeted exterior steps, walked through the glass doors and into the lobby. The interior fairly shimmered with the light from an enormous crystal chandelier that hung over the center of the vast carpeted room.

Heads turned as the handsome couple passed

52

through the area and glided up a spiral staircase that led to the second-floor restaurant. Laura knew that it was one of the finest in Miami catering to the tastes of the beautiful people from all over the world, having gained a reputation for fine food and intimate dining.

Bone china and ornate silverware gleamed from the pale blue linen cloth that covered the small table, aglow with candlelight. A waiter dressed in a black tuxedo bowed and presented Brad with an elegantly embossed red menu.

The sweet smell of fresh flowers mingled with the aromas of rich cream sauces, spicy meat dishes, and flaky dessert pastries. Laura tried hard to immerse herself in the lush surroundings, to concentrate on Brad's words, on the delicious food, on the music of the strolling violinists. But it was no use. Try as she would, she couldn't escape into the atmosphere of the evening. Or into Brad's company.

She'd done it all before. Had it all before. The surroundings, the glamour, the empty existence. She felt out of kilter. Out of sync. She couldn't help remembering the bright green afternoon she'd spent in Greynolds Park with Michael. The way the shafts of golden sunlight had played over his black hair. The quiet peaceful feeling she'd known just walking next to him along the leaf-strewn, sun-flecked paths.

She couldn't seem to become involved with her date with Brad. Her body was there, but her mind wasn't. She was listening, but she wasn't hearing. And it didn't get any better when Brad took her up to the supper club where a famous comedian was performing. The man's jokes sounded crude and humorless. His routine gave her no pleasure.

At one point in the evening, Laura realized that Brad had stopped talking. Instead, he was leaning back in his chair, staring at her. "You know," he ventured. "I'm not used to boring my dates to death."

She looked at him quickly and felt her face flush. "I-I'm sorry, Brad," she said sincerely. "I know I'm rotten company. It's not you. You've shown me a lovely evening. Please forgive me . . ."

"Come on," Brad said, taking her hand and standing abruptly. "Let me take you someplace where we can be alone. I'm tired of this guy's ramblings anyway."

She rose and followed him quickly out of the club, down in the elevator, outside, and into the car when the valet arrived with the cream-colored vehicle. Brad drove in silence, glancing over at her every now and again. Finally, he pulled into his assigned parking space at his high-rise condo.

"Come up with me," he urged. "I'll put some music on. We can talk and *really* get acquainted."

She hesitated. But the look in Brad's eyes urged her to follow him up to his penthouse apartment. Once inside, she looked around expectantly. The suite was a man's abode, masculine, modern, sleek, decorated in colors of navy and tan, brightened with peach and kelly green accent pieces. Laura thought it resembled a magazine layout more than a home—polished and perfectly arranged, yet also sterile and cold, lacking an atmosphere of homeyness.

One entire wall consisted of sliding glass doors that led out to a curved, tiled balcony. It, in turn, overlooked the sparkling jewellike glitter of the city below. They stood on the balcony and the night air settled around them, quiet and balmy. A fresh breeze fluttered across Laura's bare arms.

"Wait here," Brad whispered into her ear. His warm breath against her skin caused a shiver to race up her back. He left her on the balcony, returning a few minutes later with the sounds of soft music trailing from inside the suite.

He took her into his arms, pulled her close, and danced her slowly around the balcony. The nearness of him caused her pulse to race. His arms tightened around her. She could feel his lean body against her soft contours, then the warm pressure of his mouth on her throat. "Laura . . . Laura . . ." he whispered. "You are so beautiful . . ."

She responded to him. At least her body did. She trembled slightly and raised her mouth to his. But though her body awakened to his kisses, her mind did not. It was as if she were standing outside herself, on another part of the balcony, watching. As if she were viewing the two people embracing with a curious, almost scientific interest. It was always that way. Her body longed to know the fulfillment of physical love. If only she could give herself to Brad . . . to his desire for her.

And then, another memory floated across the landscape of her mind. She saw the face of Michael Raintree. And in that slice of time, she knew that she could not give herself to Brad—or to any man—until she had confronted her longing for Michael. Until she had met head-on the challenge and the promise of his words.

Like a moth to a flame, she was inescapably drawn to Michael. And like it or not, she had to deal with this attraction before she could go on with her life.

Brad dropped his arms. "I'm not used to turning a woman off with my lovemaking," he said coolly. "I'm better than that." In the pale light, Laura could see his eyes, grown hard.

She took a deep breath and shook off the vestiges of her own passion. Her voice was barely audible when she finally spoke. "Forgive me," she whispered. "It isn't you, Brad. Please believe me . . . it's me. I need to work out some personal things."

A flicker of anger crossed his handsome features, a twitch of controlled animalism. She recoiled slightly. Then the look was gone. "I understand," he told her in a voice that belied his words. "But you know something, Laura?" He paused, then continued. "You're worth waiting for. I've never met a woman like you. And I want you. So . . . I'll wait until you're ready."

"I-I can't promise you anything . . ." Her thoughts whirled in uncertainty.

"I said, 'I will wait'!" he restated emphatically. She turned, intending to leave the balcony. He caught her arm, squeezing it a little too tightly. She winced. "But I won't wait *forever*." It was more a warning than a promise.

She nodded mutely. Then he kissed her lightly on the cheek and led her out of his apartment, out of the towering concrete building, and into the night.

Laura sat in the Mission, listening to the rich sound of Michael's voice. The simplicity of his message filled her with both encouragement and sadness. *A strange mix,* she thought. Yet, it was true.

She felt inspired to seek a closer relationship to God for herself. But she also felt a kind of regret that she lacked a basic knowledge of how to draw closer to Him. Was Michael Raintree the key to her own personal encounter with the Lord? How did one go about "turning one's life over" as Michael encouraged his listeners to do? And what about this heartfelt attraction she had for the man himself? How could she reconcile her feelings for Michael with her feelings for the world he represented?

She had no love for the poor and elderly who sat all about her in the room. She felt sorry for them, but she had no wish to involve herself in their lives. She'd always had everything money could buy—every luxury, every protection. And now, some man, a preacher, whose congregation seemed to be the entire Third World, had intruded into her safe and private little universe and shown her a life of commitment . . . of serving selflessly, a life-giving and life-changing

Deity who seemed interested in her . . . and in what she did.

Frankly, she was frightened. And confused. And the only thing that seemed to be holding her together was also the very thing that was tearing her apart . . . Michael Raintree.

As Laura sat there, rummaging through her churning emotions, she suddenly felt the effect of eyes boring into her. Squirming in the chair, she glanced around the room for the source. She found it on her first try. Chris Avery stood against one of the walls, staring straight at Laura. Laura shifted restlessly under the unrelenting gaze.

Chris's dislike for her showed every time Laura entered the Mission. While it troubled her, she refused to be intimidated. She had as much right as anyone else to be there. So what if Chris suspected her motives for coming to hear Michael? *I don't owe her any explanations!* she thought hotly.

Laura shot Chris a look of haughty disdain and Chris answered her in kind. Well, at least their feelings for each other were out in the open! Chris didn't like Laura and Laura didn't like Chris.

But how did Michael feel about Chris? She was, after all, a beautiful woman. And a woman who already knew what God wanted from her. She had purpose. She had a place in Michael's life, serving him and the people he loved.

Laura sighed and focused her full attention on Michael. He was the key to all her tomorrows. She knew it instinctively. His presence was a safe harbor; his words, a beacon; his eyes, an open challenge to her storm-tossed emotions.

"Could we go for a ride?" Michael had whispered the question in her ear before the throng of people clustered around him. Startled, Laura had nodded mutely and then waited for the moment they could leave together. It finally came. And now they were speeding down the moonlit road with the only sounds, the wind and the low hum of the car's engine.

Michael gripped the wheel and the sports car responded to his commands. Laura rode, lost in the rush of the wind and the pale white light of a full moon. The highway stretched ahead like a gray-white ribbon. Water, bounded by shrubs and mangroves streaked by on either side of the road.

She didn't know where they were going. She wasn't sure Michael knew, either. It didn't matter. She didn't care. It was enough to be with him. Enough to have the wind and the moonlight and velvet blue-black night around them.

There was little traffic on the highway—only an occasional truck, which Michael would pass quickly. They slowed once as another car started to pull out ahead of them, and Laura caught a sign from the corner of her eye. It read: "Islamorada." They were halfway to Key West!

The long, high-speed drive seemed to be having a tranquilizing effect on Michael. The tension had gone out of his face. His convulsive grip had gradually loosened on the steering wheel. He was deep inside his own thoughts. She didn't want to intrude on them, so she rode next to him and gave herself up to the contentment of being with him.

They sped across the Seven-mile Bridge while Laura watched the moon trail a pale white path over the gently lapping water. It sunk lower and lower on the horizon. Once over the bridge, they continued to race headlong into the night across several small islands linked by shorter bridges.

Finally, they encountered a traffic light and a sign that announced: "Welcome to Key West." They had been driving four hours and had reached the last city at the tip of Florida. It was five AM.

Michael slowed and wound his way cautiously

through the quiet, empty streets. Quaint old wooden buildings with their distinctive tin roofs lined the residential streets of the town. Then, in the graying colors of predawn, the car's headlights reflected off a large stop sign that appeared dead center in the road.

Michael slowed even more, then halted the car completely. He got out, walked around the car, and opened Laura's door. It felt good to stretch her legs. She shivered in the cool air. Michael led her to the foot of a large metal sign that rose adjacent to the stop sign at the end of the road where a sea wall held back the softly slapping waves below them.

"We ran out of road," Michael said quietly. They were the first words he'd spoken in hours.

"So it seems . . ."

"Do you know where you are?"

Laura read the sign aloud. " 'The Southernmost Point in the U.S.A., Key West, Florida' . . ." She crossed her arms and squeezed herself, to stop her slight shivering. Another smaller signboard declared, "Cuba—90 miles." An arrow pointed south. "It looks as if I'm at the end of the world . . ." she whispered.

He looked down at her. In the gray morning light his eyes appeared as deep hollows. The shadow of his beard darkened his face even more. "You know," he began, "Jesus said that the kingdom of God was like a merchant's searching the world for fine pearls. One day, when he discovered a pearl of great price, he promptly sold everything he had in order to buy it."

Something stirred inside her. He was telling her something very important. Yet she couldn't quite grasp it. "These past few days . . ." she said hesitantly. "It-it's all been so complicated . . ."

"God is not complicated," he said. "He's really very simple. You're a seeker, Laura," Michael said gently. "It takes one to know one," he finished.

She gazed up at him and once again felt the

overwhelming urge to melt into his arms. If only he would hold her! She longed to feel his arms around her. Longed to lay her cheek against his chest. To have him stroke her hair and whisper her name. *Michael . . . Michael . . .* her mind cried.

But he didn't move. Instead, he whispered, "Laura . . . I don't need any complications in my life . . ."

His words stung. Was that what she was to him? A complication? She wanted to say, "But I need you in my life, Michael." Instead, she shrugged and said, "I know what you mean. I don't need any complications either. So, now that we are agreed, what next?"

Her heart pounded and she trembled on the brink of her desire for him. "I think," he said lightly, thrusting his hands in his pockets and squaring his broad shoulders, "that we should have breakfast, fill up the car, and head back home."

She nodded numbly and forced herself to say, "Good idea! I'm really starved."

As Michael helped her back into the car, he smiled. "Thanks for coming with me. It was a long drive, but exactly what I needed."

"Anytime," she said with forced brightness. But inwardly, she felt hollow. She resolved silently to give up foolish fantasies about Michael. He had a great purpose to his life. And if all she ever did for him was provide a sounding board, it would be enough. It would have to be!

They had breakfast at the end of a pier, in an old weather-beaten restaurant facing the open sea. The sleepy-eyed waitress brought them mugs of steaming coffee, a mound of smoked shrimp, and fried eggs with smoked kingfish.

"Bet you've never had this breakfast menu," Michael joked across the rough wooden table.

"It's delicious," Laura told him, peeling a fat shrimp. "And you're right. It makes caviar and fresh melon seem so ordinary!" she teased.

He laughed aloud. His eyes twinkled and her pulse raced in spite of her resolve to remain unaffected by him. They talked easily for an hour. The waitress kept their coffee mugs filled while pier regulars and fishermen, smelling of salt brine and fish, drifted through the small restaurant. Laura felt herself relaxing, and in spite of the coffee, felt the warm fingers of sleep reaching out for her. She'd been awake all night. Once home, she'd have to face Mac. She pushed that thought out of her mind and noticed Michael glancing at his watch.

"I need to make it back to Miami before noon," he said. "I'm the guest speaker at the Christian Businessmen's meeting today."

It was already seven o'clock. "We've got five hours."

"We'd better get going then." Yet, neither of them moved. He looked deeply into her eyes and she cursed herself as the old yearnings stirred within.

"You're good for me," he said quietly. "Thanks for being here."

She lowered her eyes before they betrayed her. Then they left, walking hand in hand out into the fresh, salt air of the early morning. Seagulls circled overhead, flinging their lonely cries at the sky.

Laura wished she could stop time. She allowed the colors and the sounds and the smells of the moment to seep into her consciousness, willing herself to record them all. And she locked the impressions away in her heart as the sun climbed, jewel-bright, into the heavens.

# CHAPTER 5

"ENOUGH, LAURA! I have a right to know!" Mac said, banging the top of his mahogany desk with his fist. He glared at his daughter, his eyes flashing with anger.

Laura stood in front of him, her arms crossed defiantly. She tossed her mass of hair. "I'm a grown woman, Mac!" she snapped. "I don't have to account for my whereabouts!"

He stood up and leaned across his desk. His face was flushed; his lips, pale and tight. He reminded her of an enraged bull. "You *owe* me an explanation," he said hotly. "My daughter does not disappear for one whole night without a word to anyone . . . and then expect me to act like nothing has happened!"

It occurred to her that in all her years as an adult, Mac had never raised his voice with her. How ironic. Of all the times he could have ranted, with perfect justification. Growing up, she and Monica had been guilty of their share of adolescent misdemeanors. But not this time. She might be accused of poor judgment, perhaps, but nothing more.

Laura sighed and dropped her eyes. The anger

drained away. She had no real desire to fight with her father. "Actually, Mac," she said wearily, "I went to church."

He looked momentarily stunned. "You . . . what?" he asked deliberately.

Laura felt bone-weariness creep through her. She hadn't slept for almost twenty-four hours. As soon as she had dropped Michael back at the Mission, she'd hurried home, bathed, changed, freshened her make-up, and headed for the office. Since she had to face Mac sooner or later it would be best to get it over with, so she could go back home and sleep the rest of the day.

"It's a long story . . ." She sank into the leather wingback chair at the side of his desk.

"I have all afternoon," he said firmly and sat down in his own leather chair behind his desk. A bank of clear glass windows rose behind him, framing the blue Miami sky. Laura thought it gave him the appearance of a god, sitting at some celestial judgment seat. He pressed his fingertips together and squinted at Laura through narrowed eyes.

She began slowly, choosing her words cautiously. She wanted him to know about Michael, but not about her confused feelings for him. Therefore, she gave him a factual detailing of the time she'd spent with Michael from the very first time she'd seen him. She described the Mission. She told about the people she'd met over the past few days. She spoke about Michael's unique presentation of the gospel, of his extraordinary gift of communication, of his ability to hold listeners spellbound with his voice as well as his message.

"So . . ." she finished, "when he asked me to go for a drive with him . . . I did. We drove for hours. The next thing I knew, we were in Key West. We had breakfast, then came home. That's all there was to it."

"You could have phoned," Mac said.

"You're right. I'm sorry. I should at least have phoned."

He continued to scrutinize her thoughtfully. She closed her eyes and pressed her head against the leather upholstery. She wished the inquisition were at an end. She needed to get some sleep, to be ready to see Michael again that night.

"A preacher, huh?" His question was revealing. "You find a preacher—a Bible-spouting, dirt-poor preacher—attractive?"

Her eyes flew open. Her face flushed hotly. Mac was a keen judge of human nature. He already knew far more about her feelings for Michael than she had intended to reveal.

Laura came to her feet in one quick, evasive motion. "I really *am* tired, Mac," she said, purposely avoiding his question. "I'd like to go home now. Can we talk more at dinner?"

"Of course," he said crisply. She crossed the carpeted floor and reached for the doorknob. "You know, Laura," he reminded her. "your mother and I are curious about anyone you find interesting. About anyone you think is special."

Her cheeks burned. She had wanted Mac to believe that Michael was only a minister—that he meant nothing to her. Yet, her father had deduced her emotions about Michael by simply comparing her litany of the facts with her impersonalized style of delivery. It wasn't what she told him that mattered as much as what she had *not* told him.

"If you're going to be seeing this man on a regular basis, we want to meet him. Bring him home." It was a command, thinly disguised as a request. "Plan on it. I want to meet this Michael Raintree very much."

She nodded, rankling at his edict in silent acquiescence, then quickly left her father's office.

Laura leaned persistently against the doorbell of Monica's apartment. She knew Monica was home. It was eleven o'clock in the morning. Surely she was awake by now, Laura thought impatiently. At last her persistence paid off as the door was flung open and a very sleepy, half-robed Monica stood teetering in high-heeled satin slippers.

"Stop it!" Monica barked hoarsely. "Have you no respect for the dead?"

Laura entered the apartment while Monica staggered toward the sofa and flopped down, pushing her sleeping mask higher atop her forehead.

"What time is it anyway?" Monica mumbled.

Laura surveyed the apartment. It lay in complete disarray. Empty glasses, plates littered with food, and ashtrays filled to overflowing were strewn everywhere. Cushions cluttered the floor. The mammoth marble fireplace was deep in shards of broken glass.

"Good grief!" Laura cried. "What happened? It looks like you declared a war here last night."

Monica shrugged and pressed the backs of her hands to her eyes. "Just a little party. I tried to invite you. But you were nowhere to be found." Her voice held a note of reprimand.

Laura wrinkled her nose in disgust. "I'm glad I missed it," she said. "It seems as if you entertained animals . . ."

"The maids will be here after noon." Monica yawned. Then she groaned, "Oh, my aching head!" She tugged her ivory satin negligee tighter around herself, covering her voluptuous figure. "Do be a luv," she said to Laura. "Go find me a glass of tomato juice . . ."

Laura maneuvered her way into the kitchen. It, too, was a total disaster. She tugged open the refrigerator door and peered inside. She saw three bottles of wine, a magnum of champagne, an unopened carton of yogurt, and a can of tomato juice. Laura quickly washed out a glass and filled it with the thick red liquid.

"Here," she said to Monica, handing her the glass and sitting down on the sofa next to her.

Monica sipped the juice with a grimace, and then leaned her head back against the cushion. "We missed you," she told Laura. "Brad stopped by," she added, giving her friend a sidelong glance. "He hung around for a while, like he was waiting for someone. But when you didn't show up, he left."

Laura automatically felt defensive. Of course, she'd been at the Mission the night before. Not that Michael had paid much attention to her. Ever since their ride to Key West, he'd seemed busier than ever. He was polite to her, but very preoccupied with his work.

She had tried to convince herself that he was not slighting her. But it hadn't helped. She missed the sheer presence of his company more than she ever imagined she could. Chris, on the other hand, stayed very close to him, acting almost like a layer of insulation between Michael and the demands of the people.

Lisa remained the only bright spot. The woman was consistently charming, kind, and friendly to Laura. It helped.

"Brad's very taken with you, you know," Monica added.

Laura jerked herself back to the present. "I told him not to wait around. I'm not sure what I want right now . . ."

Monica removed the sleeping mask and tossed it onto the coffee table in front of the sofa. "Tell me," she probed, "are you still infatuated with that preacher?"

Laura took a deep breath. She wanted to explain her feelings for Michael, but she wasn't sure that she could. "He's the most dynamic, interesting man I've ever known . . ." she said. "But there's more to it than that. It's what he *is*. What he represents . . ." her voice trailed. "It's the kingdom of God . . . " she added softly.

"You mean heaven?" Monica asked, raising one eyebrow skeptically.

"No . . ." Laura hesitated. "No . . . as I understand it, heaven comes later—after death. The kingdom of God is here and now."

"Where? I've never heard of such a place," Monica puzzled.

"Well, it's not really a place. It's more a state of mind." Laura struggled to put these new concepts into words. "It's . . . it's how you make choices and decisions. It's how you live your life, whom you serve, and what you're committed to . . ." she paused. "If you live in the kingdom of God, then everything else will belong to you."

Monica stared hard at her. "You've lost me," she said finally, plopping her head back against the cushion. "As far as I can tell, you already have everything there is. You've got looks, money, position . . . Good grief, what else is there?"

Laura didn't quite know how to answer her friend, and it frustrated her. "Well," she said abruptly, "I think I should get out of here and let you pull yourself together."

"Thanks," Monica sighed. "I'm not going to be fit company for the rest of today, anyway. Let's plan on lunch tomorrow, okay?"

"Sure," Laura smiled. She patted Monica's shoulder, then stood and headed for the door. Monica shut her eyes again. Laura paused at the door briefly and glanced back at the woman and the disarranged, littered room. Somehow it seemed symbolic of the chasm between them—like a great gulf with no bridge across it. She left quickly.

Laura was nervous. She surveyed herself in her full-length mirror for the tenth time that night. Her dress was both understated and elegant. It fell in a soft A-line cascade from her bust, a jade green silk with a ruffle around the high neckline and matching ruffles around both wrist-length sleeves.

Michael was coming for dinner. She felt like a schoolgirl preparing for a first date. She slipped on a string of matched pearls, removed them, then put them on again. They gleamed with their own natural luster against the solid color of the fabric.

When the doorbell rang, she still didn't feel ready, but she quickly left the room, descended the staircase, and found Michael standing in the marbled foyer, admiring the paintings and sculptured pieces lining the walls.

He smiled at her and she felt the old familiar tingle shoot through her when she encountered his penetrating blue eyes. She had wondered if he would look out of place in the luxurious surroundings of her home. But he didn't. Instead he looked as much a part of her world as she did.

"Welcome," she said, taking his hand in hers and leading him into the sunken living room. "Mother and Dad will be down in a minute."

"I like some of the art in here," he told her. "Especially the big oil in the foyer."

She was surprised. He had a good eye for art. That particular painting had been bought in the early seventies from a then-struggling artist who had since become noted and acclaimed for his work.

"I'm glad you could come," Laura said, almost shyly. "I know you're busy . . ."

"I've looked forward to this," he told her, his eyes locking with hers.

She felt her cheeks flush under the directness of his gaze and once again she felt that she was an open book and her life was a page of very readable print.

"Good evening, Mr. Raintree." The voice belonged to Mac. Both Laura and Michael turned to greet her parents as they swept into the room. Mac was a big man. But Michael was taller, slimmer, and equally broad-shouldered.

The two men shook hands, Mac's eyes never leaving Michael's face. Laura hoped that her father's blatant appraisal wasn't too obvious.

"Mr. Garland," Michael said, returning the older man's handshake.

"Please!" Mac boomed. "Call me Mac. Everyone does."

Michael nodded, greeting Ellen with a gracious compliment. Laura noted that her mother looked especially elegant and lovely. In an insightful flash, Laura realized that her bringing Michael home to meet her family was truly a big step. She hadn't brought anyone special home for dinner since college days. She smiled ruefully. She hoped Michael didn't feel like a scientific specimen.

"Laura tells us you're a minister," Ellen said. "It must be fascinating work. Whatever caused you to choose the ministry?"

A small smile tugged at the corner of Michael's mouth. "One doesn't choose the ministry, Mrs. Garland," he said gently. "The ministry chooses you."

At that moment, dinner was announced. The foursome entered the dining room. Laura saw at a glance that nothing had been spared for the occasion. The table, the silver candelabra, the place settings . . . everything matched to perfection the mood of the evening. Michael was surrounded by the Garland wealth and opulence. Mac had engineered it purposely.

Laura took a deep breath and settled into her velvet-cushioned dining chair next to Michael. Mac sat at the head of the table; her mother, across from them. Laura took a long sip of her ice water and wished she felt calmer—wished she could relax and enjoy the meal instead of having her stomach tied in knots. Yet, she noticed that Michael seemed quite relaxed and very much at ease.

"Tell me, Michael," Mac asked as Inez served lobster bisque in shell-shaped plates. "What denomination are you?"

"None, actually," Michael said. "I work under the umbrella of many church organizations. But my ministry is independent of any one group."

"Well, how do you earn a living?" Mac asked, not even bothering to disguise the directness of his question. Laura shot him an angry look. He ignored her.

"It's a fair question," Michael said. "A number of churches have pledged monthly amounts that they send me for my work. It pays the basic bills—rent, food, utilities, travel expenses. In addition, I receive royalties on a couple of theological books I've written. In short, God provides."

Mac eyed him skeptically. "And if He doesn't provide?" he needled.

"Then I didn't need it in the first place," Michael told him. Their eyes held—Michael's, open and challenging; Mac's, stubborn and tenacious.

"You must do a great deal of traveling," Ellen interceded quickly.

Michael turned to regard her. "Yes . . ." he said. "I've never been any one place more than a year."

A pang shot through Laura. It had never occurred to her that he wouldn't always be at the Mission.

"Where will you go from here?" she asked.

"I don't know yet," he said.

Laura's appetite failed her completely, in spite of the thick slice of succulent roast beef placed on the plate before her.

Sensing her daughter's inner pain, Ellen ventured,

70

"Laura tells me you've studied in Europe. Mac took me there years ago. I found it lovely and so picturesque. All those wonderful shops and marvelous things to buy. How did you find it?."

"Very old and very beautiful," Michael told her in his deep rich voice. "Actually it was a religious sojourn for me," he said. "I wanted to see the old cathedrals, visit the birthplaces of Protestantism and Puritanism . . . See where the battles started that revitalized the early church."

"A strange thing for a man to do who isn't even a part of the organized church," Mac noted.

Laura glared at him again.

"And what did you discover?" Ellen probed.

"A kind of isolationism between God and His people," Michael told her. "A feeling that the fire and power that fueled the early church had gone out. I don't believe that," he added with conviction. "God is a living fire, and it's up to the church to spread it throughout the world. Spreading the gospel wasn't a request that Christ made of his disciples. It was a command."

"A noble goal," Mac interjected. "How fortunate for God that you're willing to help Him . . . and that the church is willing to pay your way." His sarcasm dripped transparently from his tone.

Laura grew incensed at Mac's innuendo. Her hands began to shake. How dare Mac question Michael's integrity!

But Michael only leveled his violet-blue eyes at Mac and said simply, "How fortunate for me that He has considered me worthy to do His work."

The two men regarded each other, reminding Laura of proud but wary lions. She couldn't help wondering if Mac could see the reflection of his own soul within Michael's eyes the way she often had seen her own. For his own sake, she hoped he did.

The rest of the evening went more smoothly, with

71

Ellen's cleverly steering everyone clear of the topic of religion. Laura felt relief when it didn't come up again and grateful to Ellen for her deft handling of the flow of conversation.

Michael entertained them with stories of his travels—his adventures in Europe and his journeys across the United States. He had a flair for storytelling that held everyone's attention—even Mac's. Laura wished that she could slip out to be alone with Michael, but as the evening progressed, it became apparent that Mac didn't intend to let either of them out of his sight.

After she had told Michael good night, Laura returned to the patio where Mac and Ellen sat, looking out over the pool, shimmering internally with pale yellow underwater lighting. She took a deep breath and marched out onto the patio to confront her father.

"I hope you enjoyed giving Michael the third degree," she snapped.

"Calm down," Mac said. "I only asked a few questions over dinner . . ."

"Questions!" Laura exploded. "You treated him like *he* was the main course! I don't appreciate it, Mac."

He glared back at her. "You're my daughter, Laura. I want to know who you see, where you go, and what you're doing . . ."

"You acted like he was going to abduct me!"

"Face reality, Laura," Mac commanded coldly. "You're a very wealthy, very eligible young woman. There are men in this world who will take advantage of that."

"Thanks for the vote of confidence in my ability to judge character!" she retorted.

"I'm not accusing your Mr. Raintree," Mac told her. "But I think you should face facts. That kind of man does exist. And another thing," Mac added before she could sputter a rebuttal. "I don't like your going down to that Mission one bit. It's full of unsavory people who would harm you if they knew who and what you are."

Mac stood and stretched. "If you're so hot to attend church, then go to ours more often. I give enough money to it each year that we could have our names engraved on the pews if you'd like." Mac slipped off his dinner jacket and started for the French doors, marking the end of the conversation.

"I'm going up to bed," he said with a yawn. "Ellen?"

His wife nodded. "In a minute . . ." she told him. Mac left and Ellen turned to Laura, reaching out for her daughter's hand. "Laura . . . honey," she said gently. "Mac doesn't mean to be cruel. He really does have your best interests at heart."

Laura fought to hold back tears of anger that brimmed in her green eyes. "If it's worth anything," Ellen added thoughtfully, "I certainly understand why you're attracted to Michael. He's not only handsome, but certainly the most fascinating man I've ever met."

Laura looked quickly into her mother's face. Impulsively, Ellen added, "Be careful. A man like Michael doesn't live by the rules you're used to. Don't get hurt." The intensity in her voice made Laura swallow her words of retort.

Ellen kissed her lightly on the cheek and went inside. For a long time after the house grew quiet for the night, Laura sat on the patio, staring into the water. She watched the surface of the pool ripple in the soft night breeze and the light patterns dance. She sought to calm herself—to understand why she felt so keenly disappointed that the meeting between Mac and Michael hadn't gone more smoothly.

Two men. She cared for both of them. They represented two different worlds—two opposite poles. And she was being pulled apart—drawn to the one by her bloodlines; to the other, by a bittersweet yearning for . . . something more.

For as long as she could stand it, Laura stayed away from the Mission. She kept busy with her job, attended a few parties, and even accepted dinner and theater engagements with her old crowd. Once, Brad took her to lunch. They had a pleasant time, a quiet meal in a genteel continental restaurant, a warm, comfortable conversation, a sharing of good company.

Brad had kissed her lightly on the cheek afterward, squeezed her hands and looked seriously into the depths of her eyes and said, "I'm still waiting, Laura." She had been unable to say anything encouraging, yet was aware that she still found him both fun to be with and attractive.

But in the end she did return to the Mission. She arrived one late spring evening just as Chris was finishing a song in her beautiful, lilting style. Laura sat in the back, trying hard not to focus on Michael as he preached. She tried to concentrate on his message rather than his towering physical presence in the front of the room. It was a losing battle.

Lisa came over to Laura quickly when the service closed and beamed. "How good to see you again, Laura. Have you been ill? I've missed you around here."

"Me, too!" Billy Powell agreed, coming up next to Lisa and encircling her waist with his arm. Laura envied their apparent happiness. They seemed so perfect for each other; so attractive together; so very much in love. "Next to Lisa, you're the prettiest thing in this room," Billy drawled. "This place sure needs you to light it up!"

"You silver-tongued devil, you," Laura chided. "I'll bet you say that to all the girls."

"Naw," Billy said. "Only to the young ones."

Laura looked around. "Well, that's comforting. Next to Lisa, I'm about the *only* young one." The three of them laughed easily. Laura's pleasure was short-lived, however. Chris Avery joined the group, her waist-length hair cascading behind her. She raised an eyebrow and leveled her cool gaze at Laura.

"I'm surprised to see you," she told Laura. "I didn't expect you back."

Laura's guard went up immediately. "I've been busy," she started defensively. "But I never grow tired of Michael's messages. And believe it or not, I've missed some of the people I've met here."

The two women surveyed each other warily. "Michael tells me that you're very wealthy," Chris said.

It was a remark calculated to hurt. It did. Laura felt a rush of anger. Chris had made it sound as if Michael had come back and reported in to her. As if he shared details of his private life with her. Laura wondered.

"My father is very wealthy," Laura returned coolly. "I work for a living."

"In your father's business, I believe," Chris retorted. Her eyes had grown hard, and bright patches of color had risen to her cheeks.

Billy Powell shuffled and cleared his throat, perceiving the tension between the two women.

"If I read the Bible correctly," Laura parried, "wealth is not a sin." Her voice trembled slightly in her effort to control her anger.

"Correct," Chris said. "But for your own good, please realize that Michael doesn't have time to indulge some pampered, spoiled little rich girl who is bored and searching around for some way to fill up her evenings . . ."

"Chris!" Lisa cried incredulously.

Chris pressed her lips together firmly, turned on her heel, and stalked off. Laura ground her heel into the linoleum floor.

"Oh, Laura!" Lisa cried, reaching out for Laura's

arm. "I'm so sorry! I know she didn't mean it. Please, forgive her . . ."

Billy also expressed concern over Chris's outburst. "I don't know what got into her," he said. "Chris isn't vicious and mean."

"It's all right," Laura told them both, trying to gather her seething emotions. "Really. Forget it. And please, don't trouble Michael with it. I'm sure Chris and I can work out our differences."

Grudgingly Laura had to admit that what they'd said was true. She'd watched Chris minister and pray with people in the Mission too many times not to know that her cruel words and sharp tongue were not reflections of the inner woman. Chris had too much compassion, too much charity to be as perverse and contrary as she presented herself to Laura. No, Chris disliked her because, for some reason, she considered Laura her rival for Michael.

A sardonic smile played across her mouth. *A rival.* If only Chris knew the truth. Michael had not so much as flirted with Laura, she was convinced that she meant nothing to him as a woman. On the other hand, she did not know what Chris meant to Michael. But she knew with feminine certainty that Chris Avery was very much in love with him.

In spite of her run-in with Chris, Laura again began attending services at the Mission on a regular basis. She couldn't help herself. Being around Michael was all she wanted. All she needed.

And while Michael was always kind to her, always friendly, he never offered her more. She longed for more. It was maddening to be attracted to someone and never able to show it. She remembered his words from their time in Key West: " 'I don't need any complications in my life . . .'" She promised herself that she would never be a complication to him. Never!

They went out driving one moonlit night, after the

meeting. Their drives had become a habit. She realized that it was his way of relaxing, and she was glad to be able to help, if only in this way. Laura sat comfortably in the car, watching Michael guide the sports car north, along the beach front road. He usually liked to drive fast on the interstate. But not this evening. He seemed preoccupied, focused on some inner dilemma.

Looking back, she remembered that all the people closest to Michael at the Mission had seemed that way. There had been an undercurrent of excitement, of tension in the place the entire night. Even Chris had been distracted.

He stopped the car, turned to Laura and urged, "Come on. Let's walk."

She followed him along the moonscaped beach, carrying her shoes and scrunching through the warm, dry sand. "It's beautiful here," she said wistfully. The gentle waves rolled onto the shore, depositing small shells at their feet, then pulling them back into the watery depths.

The moon glistened on the surface of the ocean, laying a wide white trail over the water. A hundred thousand stars twinkled down from their velvety black canvas. The only sound was the lapping, ebbing waves. Their message seemed to be: "Michael . . . Michael . . . Michael . . ."

Walking next to him, Laura felt at peace. Yet she also sensed that this was not just an idle stroll, without purpose. "You act like someone who has something to say, but doesn't know where to begin," she said intuitively.

He stopped and turned to face her. The moon highlighted his face, etching shadows along his nose and lips. A soft breeze ruffled his black hair. "Laura . . ." he whispered her name.

And then suddenly she was in his arms, not even knowing how she'd been swept there. His mouth,

77

warm and vibrant, pressed against hers. She clung to him, tasting him, wanting him . . . She felt like a desert crawler come miraculously on water—she was drowning in him.

He held her to him, igniting a slow delicious fire that spread through her body and left her trembling. Over and over his mouth sought hers . . . over and over she gave him back kiss for kiss. He caught his hands in her hair, on either side of her face, and she could feel her own blood, hot in her temples.

He broke off suddenly, cupping her face in his large hands, drawing his thumbs tenderly along her half-parted lips. She could scarcely breathe. Her legs felt weak and rubbery. Her heart throbbed with desire for him.

Very gently he pulled her to him, engulfing her in his strong arms, and rested his chin against the top of her head. She lay her cheek against his chest, feeling the fabric of his shirt on her face, filling her senses with his scent, reveling in her pleasure of him. She could hear the thumping of his heart . . . Michael's heart . . . and she knew that she wanted him more than anything else in the world.

He brought his hands to her shoulders and very gently pushed her away. "Laura . . ." he said, his voice husky with emotion. "I-I'm sorry . . . I didn't mean for that to happen . . ."

She felt as if she'd been kicked in the stomach. She wanted to cry, "But I did! Oh, Michael, I'm so glad it happened!" Instead, she sucked in her trembling breath. "It was only a kiss. No harm done . . ."

She dropped her gaze. She didn't want him to see the lie. "Laura . . ." he tried again. "I didn't bring you here to do that. It . . . it just happened . . ."

She tried to think of something clever to say to reassure him that she didn't attach any importance to their encounter. She failed. She said instead, "Why *did* you bring me here?" Knots formed in her stomach and a chill went through her in spite of the warm, balmy night air.

"I've been asked to minister in Bolivia," he told her quietly.

"Bolivia?" she asked, as if she hadn't heard correctly.

"A friend of mine, a missionary down there, has asked me to come and spread the gospel. The Holy Spirit is moving in Bolivia. In spite of the poverty, the politics, and the past, God is moving there. And He wants me to go, too."

"I see . . ." she said slowly, calmly. But she didn't see at all. Her emotions teemed within her. Doubt, fear, rejection. He couldn't go! He just couldn't! "When will you leave?" she asked, forcing the calm, inquisitive tone to her voice.

"As soon as we can arrange for passports."

Her heart hammered. "We?"

"Billy, the Singers, and two of the men converted since we've been at the Mission."

The Singers. Chris . . . Chris would be going, too! Inside her head, Laura's voice screamed, *Ask me, Michael! Ask me to come with you. You have only to say the word . . .*

But aloud, she said, "I'm sure everyone is excited . . ." She fought to steady her quivering voice. "Why bring me here to tell me? Surely, you'll be announcing your decision at the Mission."

"I wanted you to be the first to hear—because you're special," he said tenderly.

*But not special enough to go with you . . .* she thought bitterly. "What will happen to the Mission?" she asked in an effort to make small talk and to keep her emotions in check.

"Another preacher will take over," he told her. "He's a good man. The Mission will be in capable hands."

She walked ahead along the beach, not seeing for

79

the tears that brimmed in her eyes. She didn't want him to know. He fell into step beside her.

"I'm an evangelist, Laura," he reminded her gently. "That's all I'll ever be. It's my work. It's my life."

She gritted her teeth and forced buoyancy into her voice, "Well, it was thoughtful of you to tell me privately. Thank you, Michael. Of course, I'll miss you. I'll miss all of you. But as you always tell us, 'God has His purposes.' If you have the time, will you write me a line?" she asked. Then she added hastily, "just so I can keep track of all of you ."

"Yes," he said tersely. They walked a while longer down the deserted, lonely beach before Michael said, "We'd better get back."

She turned abruptly and started toward the car. Her head ached and she felt numb all over. The night had grown cold and lifeless. The moon gave the world a metallic look and the call of the ocean had turned sad and melancholy.

All at once the night sky appeared dark and unfriendly—as if all the stars had gone out. The waves washed over the shoreline. Over and over they whispered, "Empty . . . empty . . . empty . . ."

## CHAPTER 6

MICHAEL WAS GONE. And it was as if a living part of her had been torn away. There was a hole in her life, a blank space in her time . . . and try as she might, nothing she did seemed to fill them.

Laura kept busy—ruthlessly busy. She worked with maniacal devotion. Pursued new accounts with a vengeance. Spent long hours tracking down financing, appeasing clients, and talking shop. Despite the business she brought in, Mac warned, "Slow down. You're going to burn out."

But she couldn't slow down. She couldn't stop pushing herself. Because if she did, she would remember. Michael Raintree clung to the corners of her mind. She lived on the cutting edge. Beyond that edge was an abyss. So she had to keep going, keep pushing, keep running until she fell into bed so exhausted that sleep was the only recourse for her drained muscles and her spent mind.

The elements conspired against her, causing her to confront her loneliness at every turn. The smallest things—the flame-red flowers of the royal poinciana

81

trees; the way a single shaft of sunlight cut through the moss overhead and played upon the grass; the smell of fresh earth or the salty tang of the sparkling bay—became threads in an elaborate tapestry that hung on the wall of her mind, interwoven with threads of memory after memory . . . of time after time.

If only he had never held her. If only he had never kissed her. Maybe then it would have been easier to forget. But he had. And the feel of him . . . the taste of him lingered like wispy fingers of some dilatory fog that could not quite be dissipated by the sun.

She couldn't bring herself to return to the Mission either. She tried. On the few occasions when she drove past, she could see activity inside. But she couldn't force herself to stop and go in. It would have been too painful. She picked up her Bible many times and tried to find peace and comfort within its pages. But the truth was, she was angry at God. She felt betrayed and out of touch. It was cruel—to have been so close to Him once, to have felt His presence within her life—and now to be so totally isolated, so completely cut off from His presence.

*Why?* she asked herself over and over. How could Michael's going have separated her from God, too? Yet it had. She had no answers. Only questions. A hundred questions. But the answers eluded her. Always just out of reach. A carrot dangling ever beyond her fingertips, ever on the brink of tomorrow.

"You really are a drag these days," Monica chided over lunch one afternoon. "What's going on with you?"

"I wish I knew," she sighed, taking a sip of her coffee. It tasted bitter—like the dregs of her own life. She set the cup down with a clatter. "Let's get out of here."

Monica followed her friend out into the parking lot. "I have a hair appointment," she told Laura. "But I could cancel it . . ."

82

Laura gave her a half-smile and said patiently, "I have to get back to the office. Sales conference this afternoon."

"There's a party tonight," Monica ventured.

"Thanks, but no, thanks," Laura said. "I wouldn't be much fun to be around."

"Then I guess there's nothing more to say . . ."

"I'll call you later in the week," Laura offered, feeling guilty about the way she was treating her lifelong friend.

"Please do . . . I-I've missed you . . ." Laura squeezed Monica's hand, then got into her car and drove away, leaving a very dejected Monica standing in the parking lot.

The days continued to pass for Laura—one after the other in dreary succession. Monica called to say goodbye. She was going on vacation, somewhere on the Riviera. Laura only half-listened. Then she found herself truly alone, without even Monica and her idle chatter for company.

One afternoon, after she'd shuffled an endless pile of paper, Mac called her into his office. She obeyed, feeling uneasy under his probing, questioning gaze. He sat looking at her for a few minutes before he finally said, "You're working too hard."

"Yes, but look at all the money I'm making for the firm," she told him sardonically.

"I've never asked you to give your life to this company."

She nodded grudgingly. "Sorry. That was a cheap shot. The truth is, Mac, work is all I have right now."

"A sad statement from someone so young and beautiful."

"But true . . ."

"I had lunch with Dick Meyers yesterday." Mac took a different tack. "He told me that his son Brad was mooning around, too."

Laura felt her defenses rise.

Her father plunged ahead. "I'm not meddling in your private affairs, Laura. But you could do worse than Brad."

"Trying to marry me off, Mac?" she asked.

"Don't be ridiculous!" he snapped back. "But he's a good man, Laura. Bright. Articulate. On the way up. And he's got a bad case of Laura Garland, according to his old man."

"So what's the purpose of this little chat?" she asked, leveling her green eyes at him. "To advise me not to let a good man get away?"

"No," Mac said emphatically. "To suggest that you start living again. Nobody's died, you know."

"You couldn't prove it by me . . ." She stood to leave.

"Laura . . ." Mac called. She faced him squarely. "I only want what's best for you, to see you happy again."

"Happy . . ." she repeated the word. "I don't even know what that word means. I used to think that all this," she gestured around Mac's beautifully appointed office, "was happiness. I don't believe that anymore. But I can't tell you what happiness is, either. I just don't know."

Mac pushed away from his desk and walked around to face his daughter. "I have something for you . . ." he said, and fished in his pocket.

He handed her an envelope. She took it and opened it. Inside lay an airline ticket.

"What's this?" she asked, pulling out the ticket and reading: " 'Cannes, France' . . ." She looked inquisitively at Mac. His jaw was set firmly.

"Take a vacation," he urged. "You need one. Heaven knows you've earned one. Rest, relax, get some sun. Go to that film festival they're having over there."

Laura opened her mouth in protest. He stopped

her. "I mean it, Laura. I want you to go. Monica's already over there. I've made all the arrangements. Hotel, car . . . anything you want. Just go."

"But . . . but . . ." she sputtered.

"But nothing," Mac chided. "I need the tax write-off." He attempted to lighten the conversation. "Have a good time. Stay as long as you like."

She turned the ticket over thoughtfully. Maybe Mac was right. It would be good to get away. To bury the memory of Michael in neutral territory. There would be no bumping into thoughts of him every time she drove her car, or saw sunlight on the grass, or gulls circling the bay. She looked up at Mac and gave him a tired smile.

"Perhaps you're right . . ." she mused. "A vacation might do me good."

"Of course, I'm right!" Mac beamed. "Get some new clothes, get your passport in order . . . and just take off. You won't regret it," he finished.

Impulsively, she hugged him. "Thanks, Mac. I-I do need to get away."

He hugged her lovingly, then watched as she left, closing the door quietly behind her. Laura had no way of knowing that as soon as she was gone, Mac crossed quickly over to his desk and picked up his phone.

She never saw him dial nor heard him say guardedly into the receiver, "Meyers? Well, she's going." He paused. "I've done my part," he continued crisply. "Now you see to it that you do yours. And Meyers," he warned, "you be good to her. Very good. Just do whatever it takes to make her forget this Raintree fellow once and for all." And then he hung up and sat brooding at his desk for a very long time.

Laura stretched out luxuriously on the bed in her private suite. She was exhausted. Eighteen hours of travel had finally brought her to the elegant old hotel in the fashionable seaside resort of Cannes. She'd barely seen the city during the taxi ride to the hotel. But she was here at last.

She wasn't sure exactly what she was going to do with herself, but for right now, she was content to lie dreamily on the satin-covered bed and enjoy her sumptuous surroundings. The Europeans had a flair for decorating. No Formica and pressboard in these hotel suites. The room was graced by Louis XIV reproductions. Heavy brocade curtains draped one wall which led to an intimate balcony overlooking the dazzling Mediterranean. White flocked wallpaper gave the suite of rooms an old-world charm. Mac had spared no expense, Laura thought ruefully.

An enormous bowl of flowers and fruit sat on the dresser. The card read: "Enjoy! Love, Ellen and Mac." She loved her parents for their thoughtfulness. She had been pretty hard to live with lately. She shook her head, determined not to let the old memories creep into this new time and place.

Tired as she was, Laura decided to unpack. Somehow staying busy was always her safest course. She was midway through the process, when she heard a knock on her door. Laura crossed the thick, gold carpeting, turned the French-styled door handles and pulled open the door.

"Darling!" Monica shrieked, rushing in and throwing her arms around Laura. "I'm so glad you're here!"

"How'd you know?" Laura asked. "I was going to surprise you . . ."

"Oh, Ellen told my mother, who wired me . . ." Monica flitted about the room like a bright butterfly before finally lighting on the tufted sofa. "Really, luv . . ." she drawled, "your accommodations are so much nicer than mine . . . I'm positively *green* . . ."

"Come on, Monica," Laura chided, "I'll bet you have every bellman in the place waiting on you hand and foot."

"Well . . . I *have* had to assert myself a teensy bit to make sure everything is just right . . ." she let the sentence drop. "Laura, darling!" she exclaimed, jumping to her feet. "You really must come up to the penthouse with me tonight! This count is throwing the most fabulous party . . ."

"Hold it!" Laura laughed. "I came here to relax, remember? And after eighteen hours of travel, a party is not my idea of relaxing."

"Well, you're not going to be a recluse and hide away in this room the whole time, are you?" Monica pouted.

"At these prices?" Laura laughed. "Not on your life! I plan to have a ball. Let's have breakfast tomorrow and . . ."

"Breakfast?" Monica wrinkled her nose. "Laura, that's uncivilized. The film festival is in full swing. Around here people don't even get up until the sun goes down."

"Then I'll just have to have breakfast by myself," she shrugged. "I'll lie on the beach and get a fabulous tan while you get pale and wan, staying up 'til all hours."

"Ugh!" Monica said. "You're impossible! Okay. Here's what I'll do. I'll force myself to get up by noon and come look for you down on the beach. Then we'll do some shopping."

"Fine," Laura agreed. "Tomorrow it is!"

When Monica left, Laura continued her unpacking. But she was very, very tired, and allowed sleep to engulf her the minute her head touched the satin-covered pillow.


"Laura! Laura Garland!"

Surprised to hear a man calling her name, Laura paused at the tunnel entranceway from the hotel to the beach and scanned the faces of the people in the lobby. She saw him almost at once. Brad Meyers came quickly up to her, also dressed for the beach.

He scooped her up in his arms and impulsively kissed her full on the mouth. "Brad!" she gasped, pulling back. "What are you doing here?"

"What a coincidence!" he cried, giving her the full benefit of his flashing smile.

"Mac insisted," she told him. "Said I needed a vacation . . ." she stopped in midsentence. For the first time she noticed the dark-haired, bikini-clad woman standing impatiently behind him.

"Giselle," Brad said, drawing the woman to his side while still holding Laura firmly in his embrace, "this is a good friend of mine from the States."

Giselle tossed her head and gave Laura a haughty half-smile that never reached the corners of her sultry full-lipped mouth. "Be a sweetie, Giselle," he said, "and run along."

"But, Brad!" The girl's plaintive voice was thickly accented. "What about lunch?"

"Please don't let me interrupt . . ." Laura started.

"I said, 'Run along.'" Brad's voice was more insistent, and his eyes took on a hard, cruel look.

Laura recoiled slightly, feeling vastly uncomfortable. Giselle gave her a last scathing look and then pranced off in a huff. "Brad, you shouldn't have . . ." she said.

"The woman's been a pain," Brad said lightly. "I swear, every woman here is headhunting . . . you know, looking for a rich American husband."

Laura arched her eyebrow skeptically. She hadn't liked the way he had handled things, flicking Giselle aside like some bothersome insect.

"It's true," he insisted with an easy, silky laugh. "That's why I feel so safe with you. I *know* you have no such plans!"

Laura laughed aloud, allowing his charm to dissipate her apprehensions. "I'm on my way to the beach," she said. "Care to join me?"

"I was hoping you'd ask," he smiled. Then taking her arm in his, they walked out into the brilliant light of the morning, down the boardwalk and across the warm white sand.

Laura allowed Brad to see her frequently over the next few weeks. Together, they took long, leisurely drives through the French countryside. They toured an ancient fortress and climbed the winding steps to the turrets of an old castle that had stood overlooking the French coast for nine hundred years. They dined in small, countryside inns, shopped for fine French lace to send home, strolled along winding rivers.

Yet for Laura, there was no magic—no passionate desire to be with Brad always, to be a part of his life. She knew he wanted more from the relationship than she was willing to give. The first time he tried to take her in his arms, she pulled away. "I'm just not ready yet, Brad," she'd whispered.

He dropped his arms. "I'm not asking for a lifetime commitment." His voice was coldly sarcastic. "But I know you're a woman who's capable of responding. You have before," he reminded her, not too gently.

He was right. Before—she had responded to him. Before that night on the beach with Michael Raintree. Bitterly she realized that even now, on the coast of France, in the arms of another man, Michael still cast a long shadow over her life.

Much to Laura's regret, Monica stayed out of the way. Laura would have liked for them to be a foursome, but Monica dashed from one man to another, unable to sustain interest in anyone longer than a few days at a time. If Brad had not been keeping her so occupied, Laura might have worried about her.

One of the things Brad had been badgering Laura

about was a sailing trip. Never having been much of a sailor, she was somewhat skeptical. They would be alone in a boat in the Mediterranean for most of the day. But the day was so beautiful, the sea so blue, the sun so warm, that once away from the marina, she forgot her apprehension.

Brad was an expert sailor and he handled the sails and the tiller with ease. "Duck!" he cried as the boom swung across the back of the boat. Laura scrunched low and looked up in time to see the great nylon sail swing about, flutter loosely, then rapidly fill with wind.

"Bravo!" she called, feeling the exhilaration of the wind in her face and the damp sea breeze against her skin. The sun beat down, warm and golden, drying the sea spray and leaving the faint taste of salt on her lips. "This is wonderful!" she cried.

Brad smiled at her and loosened the mainsail, to slow the boat slightly. Laura could no longer see the shoreline. They seemed utterly alone in the cool blue sea. Then, just as quickly as the wind had shifted, it died completely. The sail went slack and fluttered. Brad tied it down and shrugged apologetically. "Sorry," he told her. "Be patient, it'll rise up soon. That's the crazy thing about wind. It's very unpredictable."

Laura sat in her white shorts and red cotton top, clutching her knees to herself. She felt his open, admiring gaze sweep her figure. There was something hungry in his look, and she felt a sudden need to move beyond his reach. She dropped her eyes and said, "Mind if I get some sun?"

"Be my guest," he gestured toward the tapered bow.

Laura rose quickly and carefully made her way to the front of the boat. Stretching out on her stomach, she reveled in the feel of the warm sun on her back and legs. She lay her head across her arms and listened to the lapping of the water against the sides of the vessel.

She might have fallen asleep, but she felt the boat lurch and looked up to see Brad settling himself next to her. He'd removed his shirt, revealing his hardened, tanned chest and strong, compact shoulders. He reached down and flipped her hair off the nape of her neck, exposing it to the sun's rays.

Laura drew back slightly; his touch was foreign to her. It had a possessive quality about it that made her nervous. "You're very lovely, you know . . ." he said softly. Then he bent and brushed the base of her neck with his lips.

Self-consciously she whispered to him, "Brad, . . . don't . . ."

He reached over and brought his hands down the length of her back, kneading her muscles, letting his fingers linger at her waist. "Relax," he urged. "We have all the privacy in the world. There's no one around for miles . . ."

She rose to her knees. "Don't, Brad," she said, more insistently this time.

" 'Don't, Brad,' " he mimicked. "Is that all you can ever say to me?" His eyes narrowed and she was suddenly afraid.

She rose, but he reached up, caught her wrist, and pulled her back down. "Oh!" she cried, losing her balance and falling against his chest.

He caught her tightly by both wrists, yanked her close and kissed her hard on the mouth. She twisted to free herself, but his grip was like iron. "Stop it!" she gasped.

"Why?" he demanded, bruising her mouth with another. "I want you, Laura," he said harshly, his eyes glinting in the bright sunlight. "I've been very patient, too. I've never waited so long for any woman."

She struggled as he forced her back against the solid surface of the boat's unyielding hull.

"No!" she begged, twisting and writhing under the weight of his body. "Please! Don't touch me!" Pure panic seized her. Brad had turned into an animal, pawing and clawing. She called out, but there was no one to hear her. She pushed and shoved at him, but he was like a man gone mad. He was a stranger, a demon, intent on devouring her.

She squeezed her eyes shut and sobbed, "O God, help me!" It couldn't be like this. It shouldn't be like this. Then from the pit of her terror, she found an untapped measure of strength. She got her knee up under his chest, and heaved. He was tossed back, just long enough for her to scramble out from under him.

She lunged toward the tip of the bow. "Laura!" he yelled, reaching out for her. She paused for only an instant, then dove headfirst into the blue waters. The sea closed over her, blocking out all sound. She surged forward, swimming underwater, until she felt as if her lungs would burst. She finally struggled upward, hitting the surface, gasping for air. She stroked the water with clean, strong strokes, putting as much distance as possible between herself and the boat.

"Laura!" she heard Brad scream after her. But she swam with dogged determination in the opposite direction. "Don't be a fool!" Brad yelled. "You're miles from shore! You'll drown!"

She turned and looked back over her shoulder, treading the gently rolling waves. "I'd rather drown than be alone with you!" she shot back. Her fear had given way to anger. "How will you explain this to my father, Brad?" she shouted hotly. "How will you explain to him that his daughter drowned on a perfectly windless day off the coast of France?"

He wet his lips with his tongue. The look of fear that crossed his face she recognized but didn't fully understand. Brad hastily untied the sail and released it to seek whatever wind it could find. It filled slightly. He grabbed the tiller and tried to force the boat into the wind and toward Laura. She resumed her swimming.

"Don't!" he shouted after her. "Please . . ." he added almost choking on the word. "Get back in the boat! I-I won't touch you again. I swear."

Laura stopped swimming and treaded water. She was already exhausted. Her arms felt heavy, weighted. It was true. She would never make it back to land alone. Yet, to get back in the boat with him. . . .

He managed to find enough wind to swing the boat alongside her. He stretched out his hand. She eyed it suspiciously, too exhausted now to resist. "Come on," he said curtly. "I said I wouldn't touch you."

She allowed him to pull her over the side. She lay in the seat, gasping for breath, fighting tears. Careful not to touch her, Brad tossed her a large bath towel, then sat down at the tiller and concentrated on filling the sail with the fickle wind.

Laura tugged the towel tightly around her and shook . . . with cold, with anger, with fear. The once beautiful day had turned bleak and ugly. A part of her she'd once considered burdensome had become suddenly very special and very sacred—a gift to be given out of love, never out of fear or boredom.

Brad said nothing to her all the way back to the marina. It was just as well. She certainly had nothing to say to him. By the time the docks came into view, Laura had composed herself. She determined to say only that she'd foolishly fallen overboard. Brad knew the truth. He would have to live with it.

She did a lot of thinking on the way back. She'd taken a hard look at herself, at her life, at her future. And suddenly she knew what she was going to do about it. She knew *exactly* what she was going to do.

"It's true, then. You really are leaving." The question came from Monica, who stood in the doorway of Laura's bedroom suite and watched as her friend emptied her closet and carefully laid her clothing in two neat stacks on the bed.

Laura nodded. She was concentrating on what she was doing. There was no time for idle chatter. Nor did she want to give Monica the opportunity to dissuade her.

"You're going to Bolivia, aren't you." It was a statement. Not a question.

"Yes," Laura confirmed. "I should have gone there in the first place. It's where I belong."

"With Michael," Monica said. Yet her voice held no accusation.

Nevertheless, Laura was defensive. Her nerves were raw. It had been a long, hard day. "Yes, with Michael. I know I can never explain it to you," Laura told her. "But, Monica, I want so much more than Michael. I-I wish I could make you understand . . ." Laura broke off.

Monica crossed over and sat quietly on the bed. Her eyes never left Laura's face. "I know, luv," she said softly. "You want the kingdom of God."

Laura looked at her quickly, skeptically. But there was no mocking look on her face. "Yes," Laura nodded. Perhaps Monica did understand just a little.

"I envy you," Monica whispered. "To be so sure of what it is you want. To want something so much that you'd give up everything else to get it."

Laura stopped her packing. She crouched in front of her friend, clasping both of Monica's hands in hers. "Yes!" she cried. "I know what I want. I want the world of Michael Raintree. I want to be a part of his life. A part of what he's doing. I want to know God the way Michael knows Him." Her voice was fervent, her eyes glistening. "If I never have that, I will never be whole. Never be complete. Do you understand?"

Tears shimmered in Monica's blue eyes. She nodded. "How I wish I felt that kind of passion for something. For anything . . ."

"Come with me!" she urged, holding Monica's slim fingers tightly in her grip. "Michael's world is for everyone. You can have it, too . . ."

"No," she said, shaking her head. Her voice was barely audible. "I-I can't."

"Why?" Laura pleaded. "Why can't you?"

"This," Monica said, withdrawing her hand and gesturing about the room. "I'm scared, Laura. I'm not brave like you. I can't leave all this. I wish I could . . . but I just can't."

Laura stood slowly, dropping Monica's other hand. Sadly, she knew that Monica was right. She couldn't leave it all. The price for Michael's world was too great for Monica to pay—too great.

"If you ever change your mind . . ." Laura let the sentence fade into the air.

"Sure." Monica tried to smile nonchalantly.

Laura finished her packing in silence. She snapped her suitcase shut and turned to Monica, still sitting motionless on the bed. "Will you do me a favor?"

Monica looked up dully. "Of course," she said.

"Ship these things back to Miami for me. I'll have no need of them in Bolivia."

"Do you know where he is?" Monica asked.

It took Laura a moment to comprehend her question. "La Paz," she answered. "In an inner-city Mission run by a man named Rey Ortiz. Don't worry, I'll find him."

"Your parents?"

"I'll write them," Laura picked up the phone and called for a bellman. When he arrived, she sent him ahead to the lobby with her luggage.

"Will you be all right?" Laura asked Monica hesitantly.

Again, Monica looked up at her. Fresh tears

trembled in her eyes. "Laura," she whispered. "You were my best friend. The only person who ever really cared . . ."

Laura swallowed the lump in her own throat. "If you ever change your mind . . ." she repeated.

Then she crossed swiftly to the door. There she paused and looked back at her lifelong friend. She would always remember Monica Jerrel huddled on a satin-covered bed, in a gilt-edged room, shrouded by silk and brocade and velvet. Like a butterfly in a crystal jar.


The plane was descending, knifing its way through layers of white vapor clouds. From her seat by the window, Laura observed the dark ridges of hills, brown and sparsely streaked with green. In the distance, she sighted the snowy tops of mountains jutting into blue sky—great peaks of the Andes, ancient, as old as time. The plane circled over the mountain plateau city of La Paz. She saw it sprawled out below in the bright morning sun. It was situated in a deep valley, surrounded by the mountains, like a little emerald tucked in a jeweler's cloth.

She sighed. For the first time in her life, Laura Garland was completely alone. Thousands of miles from the safe, secure world of her father. Light-years away from the person she had once been. She was apprehensive, but she wasn't afraid. What would Michael say when she walked in? How would she be received by the rest of the team? By Chris? By Lisa? They had all probably expected never to see her again.

Once she stepped outside the plane, Laura found the air thin and cool. It was difficult to breathe and she stood gasping for breath in the clear, intense sunlight. Laura shook her head and decided that jet lag was finally catching up to her. She also wondered why it seemed so cool. Then she remembered that she had passed into the Southern Hemisphere. Although it was June, in this part of the world it was winter time.

Inside the terminal, Laura exchanged her traveler's checks for Bolivian pesos. She asked the American Express office for a local directory before hailing a taxi and directing the driver to the address she'd already confirmed to be Rey Ortiz's Mission. She thought it best to start there, since she didn't know the hotel headquarters for the group.

She glanced nervously at her watch, which was still set on Cannes time. In Bolivia, it was a little past noon. She settled back in the cab and looked out the window. The air was warmer now, but still clean and refreshing, with a translucent quality that made the distant mountains seem sharp and defined. She realized that there was no haze or pollution to distort their profile.

The city was an odd mixture of the modern and the ancient, both picturesque and colorful. The streets were laid out, helter-skelter, seemingly without pattern or plan. The main boulevard was a wide, spacious avenue, lined with trees, plazas, and parks; the buildings, a blend of brick and wood; the people, small with olive skin coloring, dark hair, and dark eyes. Many were Indians, dressed in the colorful garb of their ancestral tribes—long flowing dresses and bowler-shaped hats. Vendors, with wooden carts and stands overflowing with exotic foods and trinkets, crowded every corner, hawking their wares.

The cab driver took his job seriously, driving with one foot on the accelerator and one hand on the horn. Under his breath he kept muttering in Spanish. Laura began to doubt she'd ever arrive when, suddenly, the cab came to a stop in front of a group of low storefronts on a narrow, tight little street. One front had a window with a cross painted on it, a sign in Spanish and an open doorway. The Mission!

She'd come from halfway around the world. And

now, just beyond that doorway, lay her future. Her heart hammered and her mouth felt dry. She still felt lightheaded and dizzy. Lightweight, too, as if there were no gravity to hold her down. She paid the driver, who carried her luggage into the building, set it down and left. Nervously, she glanced around. The room was empty, except for a few people clustered at the front.

Suddenly, she heard a shriek. She turned in time to see Lisa rushing toward her, arms outstretched. "Laura!" Lisa cried, throwing her arms around her. "Oh, Laura! You're here! I can't believe it!"

Laura hugged her warmly. It felt wonderful to see a familiar face, to have somebody happy to see her. "Let me look at you!" Lisa backed away, holding Laura by her shoulders.

"Who says God doesn't answer our prayers!" Lisa bubbled. "I'm *so* glad you're here!" she gasped. "You're just in time for the wedding!"

## CHAPTER 7

"WEDDING?" LAURA ASKED, her stomach somersaulting. She felt certain that all the color had completely drained from her face. The images of both Michael and Chris floated across her numbed mind.

"Are you all right?" Lisa asked, gripping Laura's arm in support.

Laura nodded and took a deep breath. She still felt giddy.

"I know what's wrong," Lisa ventured. "It's the altitude here in La Paz. The Indians call it *soroche*— mountain sickness. I felt the same way for a while when we first arrived. You're twelve thousand feet above sea level," Lisa explained. "As soon as you get acclimated, you'll be fine."

Laura smiled weakly. Of course, Lisa was right. The altitude was affecting her. But Lisa's bombshell had hit her hard, too. Screwing up her courage, she asked again, "What wedding?"

"Why, mine!" Lisa beamed. "This Saturday, in the Gardens of La Paz, Billy and I are going to be married."

The flood of relief that swept over Laura left her drained. "I'm so happy for you . . ." she cried a split second later, embracing Lisa enthusiastically.

"Michael is going to perform the ceremony," Lisa added. "And I can't think of anybody I'd rather have show up for my wedding than you!"

Laura cleared her throat and attempted to inject a casual tone into her voice. "How is Michael?"

A frown formed on Lisa's pretty pixy-like face. "That's another reason I'm glad you're here," she said. "He's working much too hard. Pushing himself beyond human endurance. He puts in fifteen- and eighteen-hour days. Billy's concerned . . . in fact, we all are. It's like he's drowning himself in work."

"Yes," Laura said ruefully. "I'm familiar with the syndrome."

"Anyway, Billy and I agreed that you seem to be the only person he's ever known who can make him relax. All those times in Miami . . . remember?"

Laura remembered. Too well. But would Michael be glad to see her here? Now? It would be better to know than to continue wondering. "Can I see him?" she asked meekly.

"Of course," Lisa said. "Our hotel is just a short walk from here. Michael and Billy are there now. It's siesta time, and nothing moves in the city until about four o'clock. Our meeting begins back here tonight at 7:30, so there's plenty of time."

"Let me get my bags . . ." Laura started for her luggage.

"Wait!" Lisa told her. "Miguel!" she called. A boy whom Laura guessed to be about thirteen years of age came forward. "Please carry these back to the hotel," Lisa instructed in Spanish.

The boy agreed and the three of them set off for the hotel. Again the thin air left Laura gasping, but the temperature was rising and the afternoon promised to be pleasant and warm.

The hotel was an old building, three blocks from the Mission. Though the lobby was rundown and the furniture, old, it was clean and quiet. Large overhead fans spun slowly, giving off a soft metallic clink. Laura waited as Lisa explained to the desk clerk that another member of Mr. Raintree's group had arrived.

"You'll have your own room," Lisa explained. "Actually, this place is owned by one of Rey Ortiz's men. They've let us have the rooms *gratis*. I've been staying with Chris. Billy, with Michael. But of course that will change Saturday . . . Billy and I will have our own room . . ." she added shyly. "The rest of our people—Jack, Phil—are staying up on the third floor."

Laura was only half-listening. Michael was *here*—under this roof. She would see him soon, would know whether or not he had missed her.

They put her bags in a small, stuffy room. Laura could not have described its appearance. She was too involved with her thoughts.

Lisa led her down the hall, pausing in front of Room 207. "I almost hate to knock," she whispered to Laura, "just in case he's resting."

All at once Laura lost her nerve. "Maybe I could check back later . . ."

"No way," Lisa smiled. "He'll want to know you're here." She knocked lightly.

"Yes?" The voice answering through the closed door was Michael's. Laura's heart pounded and her hands grew clammy.

"It's me . . . Lisa."

"Billy's gone out for a while," he called through the wooden barrier.

"That's all right," she said. "I have someone here who wants to see you."

There was a long pause. Laura's heart continued to hammer. The door opened and she was staring up into the bottomless blue eyes of Michael Raintree.

Neither of them spoke. For the briefest moment, Laura thought she saw a flicker of joy cross his handsome face. But it passed so quickly that she wasn't sure. Perhaps she had imagined it because she wanted so desperately for it to be there.

"Laura!" When he spoke her name, a shiver went through her. "Come in!"

"I'll leave you two alone," Lisa said, slipping away and closing the door behind her.

Michael stood gazing down at her and Laura smiled tentatively, not sure of what to do next. More than anything, she wanted to reach out and touch him, but she was afraid that if she did, she wouldn't let go.

Michael turned abruptly, breaking the spell. "I'm surprised to see you . . ." he said.

"I'm surprised to be here," she whispered.

He leaned against the bureau in the cramped hotel room. An overhead fan whirled mechanically, emitting a faint "whooshing" sound. He crossed his arms and surveyed her, his eyes scrutinizing her, looking through her as though she were a pane of clear glass— as though her thoughts, her heart, her soul were transparent.

She backed off slightly and walked over to a window to stare down at the traffic below.

"Why did you come, Laura?"

The moment of truth. She couldn't lie to Michael. She couldn't act nonchalant. Somehow she had to communicate to him what was going on inside her. What had been going on since the day he'd left. But she didn't want to come across like some love-sick fool either. Her nerves were taut, her words hesitant, yet they came from her innermost being.

"I had to . . ." she told him. "In Miami you gave me something I never knew existed. Do you know, I've gone to church all my life and I never knew God the way you do? No one ever told me about His kingdom . . . how it's available to His people right

102

here. Right now. I tried to go back to my old life. Tried to pick up where I left off before you . . . before God. I-I couldn't. I spent three weeks in Cannes. I was miserable . . ."

She turned to look at him, tears glistening in her eyes. "I want to stay, Michael. Please don't send me away."

His jaw clenched. He took a deep breath and closed his eyes. She watched his body tense and finally relax, is if he were fighting an inner war. Six feet of space separated them. Yet it might as well have been a chasm. When he at last opened his eyes, he said, "It's very different here, Laura. There are very few of life's amenities around here. And I haven't even gone out into the jungles yet to villages with no running water—where women still wash clothes in the piranha-filled rivers."

He paused. "Do you know that some of these jungle tribes can't even make fire? That's right," he added, seeing her startled look. "They have to steal it from one another, because they don't know how to make it for themselves. Yet these are the people I'm called by God to reveal the gospel to. And Laura, they are so hungry for His Word!" Michael's voice rose with fervor. "There's nothing here for you but long hours and hard work."

She felt her own temper begin to rise. "I'm not some hot-house flower, Michael!" she said, tossing her head. "I understand this is not a vacation on the Riviera! That's *not* why I'm here!"

He surveyed her again. "If God has truly called you to this place, then you're right. You will make it. But it's going to be tough. The food, the people, the customs . . . everything's different here. Do you understand?"

She pressed her lips together and swallowed her anger. "Yes," she said tersely. "None of it matters. I want to stay."

He held her eyes with his, measuring what he saw there. Finally, he said, "All right. If you stay, you work. What can you do?"

It was a challenge she welcomed. She was tired of sitting on the outside looking in. She wanted to give something back—to offer something worthwhile. She wanted to serve God . . . and Michael . . . and in her heart, she felt willing to pay any price.

She'd already considered her answer. "I have a degree in public relations," she told him. "I can write a newsletter for you. Maybe to send back to the States. To keep the people who support you informed . . ."

He nodded slowly, assessing her suggestion. "Yes, we need a newsletter." he agreed. "I don't have time, yet it's necessary."

Relief flooded through her. "All right," he told her, walking across the room. "It's settled. You're part of the team. I'm sure you know that Lisa is getting married. You can move in with Chris after Saturday . . ."

Panic flared within her. Chris—the *last* person she wanted to see! She licked her lips thoughtfully and offered, "Look, Michael . . . I'd rather have my own room. Really, I'm the one person here who can afford to pay my way. Don't let me be a financial drain on your ministry."

He nodded in agreement. "Very well. Unpack your things and get some rest. Be at the Mission tonight by 6:30. We expect a big crowd."

"Of course," she said briskly, suddenly all business. As he held the door for her, his hand brushed her shoulder. She jumped back, as if his touch had burned her. Then she steeled herself and hurried down the hall to her room. Once inside, she locked the door and fell onto the bed. She was drained and exhausted. But she was happy too. Deeply happy . . . and she hadn't felt happiness for months. She was staying. She was actually going to be a part of Michael's life. And it didn't matter how small a part. It was enough to be near him and the Kingdom he proclaimed . . .

"So, what I heard is true. You really *are* here." The words came from Chris. Laura paused on her way to the front of the Mission and turned to confront Chris' unfriendly gaze. It was early yet, but a steady stream of people was already arriving. Chris's was the first negative reaction she'd received since her arrival in La Paz. Phil, Jack, Billy . . . the rest of Michael's Miami group had been delighted to see her. She was beginning to feel at home, when Chris's cutting comment caught her off guard.

"Yes," Laura told Chris cautiously. "I'm here."

"Not many fancy restaurants and zippy sports cars around here," she sniffed.

Instantly Laura's temper flared, but she gritted her teeth and fought against a rising tide of sarcastic words. It wouldn't be very charitable to cause a scene on the floor of the Mission an hour before Michael was to preach. And it would serve no purpose for the two of them to continue their hostility. "I'm sorry you think that those things have value to me, Chris. Actually I came because God drew me here. I don't know why exactly. But I know this is where I belong."

Laura paused, noting the surprised look on Chris's face. Bolstered, Laura continued. "I'm not your enemy, Chris. I'm simply searching for answers for my life. I believe that Michael knows those answers."

Chris did not respond, but her gaze faltered and something went out of her, causing her to deflate like a rag doll. "I-I have to go onstage," she countered evasively. Laura watched Chris turn and hurry to the front of the room where Jack and Phil stood tuning their instruments.

105

Laura waited, taking deep breaths, knowing that she'd made an important step in dealing with Chris Avery. She also realized that while she and Chris might never be friends, they at least were no longer enemies.

The room filled quickly. Hundreds of Bolivians poured in. Billy told her that some had walked for miles to get there. She believed it. They were old, young; men, women, and children—a population consisting of Quechuas, Aymaras, Mestizos, some Europeans. There seemed to be a cross-section of lifestyles and cultures. Some were poor; yet, many were middle-class. They looked eager, hungry, yearning for hope and purpose. It dawned on Laura then, watching them arrive, that the gospel really was for everyone—even little rich girls from Miami, she told herself ruefully.

The Sonshine Singers created their beautiful music. Their gospel music. The people loved it and responded, tapping their feet in time to the rhythms. Once Michael stood up to preach, Rey Ortiz, a small, muscular man with black hair, black eyes and a pencil thin mustache, translated his message into Spanish for the hushed, enraptured masses.

Laura was mesmerized by all of it. But most of all, by Michael himself, whose fiery words and life-changing message had inspired another world, another people to come into the presence of God . . . into the covenant of His grace and mercy. Michael's salvation message swept through the hearts of the people like a wildfire, and afterwards, hundreds came forward for prayer and ministry.

By the time the meeting broke up, it was after 1:00 AM . Laura had done nothing more than watch, pray silently, and observe Michael. But her spirit soared. She had been in the presence of God, and she knew it. Like Isaiah, the prophet, she had "seen the Lord, high and lifted up." She had felt His Spirit in the room and it had been exhilarating . . . uplifting . . . beyond words. Beyond anything she had ever felt before.

Scales of doubt had fallen from her eyes. Fear had fled from her heart. She knew where she belonged. She knew where she was going. It was as if she were high atop a mountain, and the voice of God had called her to Himself. A peaceful quietness descended over her as she slipped quietly back to her room in the hotel.

She sat alone in the room, in the dark, for a very long time. A full moon shone outside in the inky Bolivian sky. She raised the window, feeling the cool night air rush in, and then sat and pondered the silver face of the moon. It had never looked more beautiful, more ethereal. She reflected back over the past few months of her life. How far she'd come! From the boardrooms of Miami, to the worldly glitter of Cannes, to the mountains of Bolivia.

Yet, she'd come so much farther inside herself. She'd shifted from harboring vague notions about an uninvolved, fatalistic God to the realization that He was Sovereign in all aspects of His people's lives. The journey had been long and sometimes difficult. She'd seen parts of herself she hadn't liked. Parts she'd never known about. But she was here at last— spiritually renewed—ready to turn control of her life over completely to God. To the Lordship of Jesus Christ. To the leading Spirit of the Holy Ghost, who shimmered ever before her as a living fire, a cleansing blaze.

Laura Garland had made the journey from an intellectual perception of God to a heartfelt devotion for Him. And if the journey were to end here, right now, on this very night, she knew that she was finally spiritually whole. She knew that she had found the kingdom of God. That she had discovered the ". . . pearl of great price." And she was determined to cherish it.

She understood that churches were people, not buildings. She perceived that God dwelled in men's hearts, not in stone and concrete edifices. And she knew that she, too, had been chosen to be a member of Christ's church body. So she vowed that she would serve Him—however He chose; however He wanted. And if that included giving up her wealth, her family, and her country, then she would. Christ was sufficient for all her needs.

Even though she was willing to make any sacrifices to live her life under Christ's banner, she was unsure of what God wanted from her as His servant. Until she knew, she would stay and work in Bolivia with Michael—because Laura realized something else as she sat gazing up at the glowing surface of the moon. She loved Michael Raintree—as a minister, as a fellow Christian, as a man. With all her heart, she loved him.


Laura had dressed carefully for the wedding. In her hasty packing as she was leaving Cannes, she hadn't thought to put in elegant dresses. But her feminine vanity had forced her to pack one special dress, a lovely cotton voile, long-sleeved, full-skirted, with a deep V neckline, encircled with a simple, fluid ruffle. It was printed in a random swirling of various shades from jade to lime to deep emerald, the pattern broken occasionally by touches of deep mauve.

She wore her hair long, caught up on one side with an emerald green comb. She left her legs bare, slim and golden, her feet tucked into low-heeled sandals. Laura looked like summer, a fragrant reminiscence of soft, watercolor days, a song that lingers in one's memory, a refrain to haunt the mind of other times . . . other places.

She sat amidst the lush green foliage and singular beauty of the Wedding Garden. The blue Bolivian sky sparkled above the small gathering of people, who, like Laura, waited for the wedding to begin. Many of the rock formations bore an eerie resemblance to the surface of the moon, grayish-white in color, stark and alien to the human eye as if locked away in time, shielded from decay by a nonfunctioning cosmic clock. A small altar, laden with cascades of white fragrant flowers, stood at the front of the Wedding Garden.

Laura fidgeted in her chair. In moments Billy and Michael would emerge. And after them, Lisa would come up the natural rock aisle, passing the congregation and joining her beloved at the altar of God. Laura had been to many weddings. Weddings of sorority sisters, college friends, high school friends. But she'd never anticipated one so eagerly.

Jack played softly on a keyboard attached to hidden electrical outlets, and then Chris walked to the front. She stood, looking bright and golden, the sunlight bouncing off her platinum river of hair. She held a guitar and then her nimble fingers plucked the strings and the crystalline air filled with her incredibly haunting voice.

Chris sang of covenants—of marriage between the Spirit of God and the spirit of man—of the blending of Spirit and flesh—of the melding of man and woman into one flesh. Her music told of life and commitment, of giving and sharing. Laura felt tears pool in her eyes as the music wrapped around her heart and touched a chord of longing deep within her.

As the final trembling notes drifted into the morning sky, Michael stepped forward. Sunlight hung in the air like taut yellow ribbons. Shafts of liquid gold flowed across his hair and shoulders. His suit was dark, perfectly cut. His black hair gleamed under the impact of the sun, while his startling blue eyes glowed with power and intensity.

Billy joined Michael at the altar and turned to watch Lisa come down the aisle on the arm of Rey Ortiz.

She looked lovely, a precious cameo in intricate lace, stepping from the pages of a storybook. Laura's own heart swelled with sisterly love for her.

The ceremony was simple and elegant. They exchanged their vows, each repeating the time-honored words after Michael. Billy slipped a thick band of gold on Lisa's finger, then raised her veil and kissed her. Jack hit triumphant chords on his keyboard, and the newly married couple hurried up the aisle.

Afterward, there was a small reception in a corner of the Garden, where foliage hung over a tiled patio and vines tangled through the latticework of a gazebo. Jack and Phil set up their amps, microphones, and instruments. Two local boys, friends of Rey, joined them and together they played upbeat, contemporary numbers for the guests. Hearing them play, Laura marveled at the pure talent the musicians possessed. She was positive that they could have pursued professional careers, but, like Michael, they had heard a higher calling and had followed it instead.

Laura hung back, on the fringes of the celebration, feeling out of place, a bit like someone observing a party through a window. Lisa and Billy were surrounded by friends; the musicians were involved with their music; Michael was in a discussion with Rey. She knew some Spanish, but not enough to communicate with anybody, so she withdrew to stroll through the gardens.

She wasn't lonely. She merely wanted to hold onto the tranquility and beauty of the day. She wanted to savor the memories of the wedding, review the weeks ahead, and ask God to reveal her place in the larger picture. Just where did Laura Garland fit in? What was God calling her to do in Michael's ministry?

She had learned already that Michael was a celebrity of sorts, with hundreds of people clamoring to hear him preach. Larger and larger arenas had to be found as the word of his evangelistic services spread. The poor and wealthy alike flocked to see him. Several world church missions and European-based missionary groups had invited him to come to the smaller cities of Bolivia to preach. Some of the areas were far from La Paz, in jungle regions. There was so much to be done! There were thousands of people—only one Michael . . .

Laura sighed, snapping herself back to the present, realizing that she needed to return to the reception. She wanted to toss rice at Billy and Lisa before they left for their three-day honeymoon to Lake Titicaca, an icy blue water crater high in the Andes. Three days. It was all Michael could spare them.

She walked quickly back toward the sounds of the music and laughter. But as she emerged from the shadows, she looked up and stopped cold, her eyes fastening on a singular couple, lost in conversation, sharing intimate laughter. Laura saw Michael and Chris—he, tall and slim and laughing with sun patterns glancing off his black hair; she, petite, delicate and golden, her head tilted up at him, her silvery hair streaming behind her.

Laura watched, hypnotized, her mind numb and her stomach fluttering. They were so beautiful together . . . a great sadness swept over her and she edged back into the surrounding shadows of the rock formations so that they would not see her. She clenched her teeth and dug her nails into the palms of her hands. A trembling sense of longing swept through her, shaking her with its power.

It would be so easy to run away. Who would miss her? Who would care? Then she remembered her vow—the one she'd made to God to serve Him. Now she had to keep it. Even if it meant losing Michael Raintree. For, like him, she belonged to Christ first.

Laura allowed her gaze to follow Chris and Michael as they walked across the tiled floor. For one brief moment, Chris looked Laura's way. Their eyes met and held. Chris acknowledged her, and warned her away, with the slightest dip of her head, the smallest upturn of her lips, the minutest flash of her eyes.

Later in her room, Laura paced back and forth like a caged animal. Her flesh battled with her spirit. In her mind's eye, all she could see were the luminous faces of Michael and Chris. Laura felt darts of jealousy pierce through her heart. For the first time in her life, Laura was actually jealous of another woman. It was not a pleasant emotion. The poet was correct: ". . . it pricked the soul with swords of doubt."

She tried in vain to revive her idealism and devotion to the God who had so lovingly redeemed her. But just now, seeing Chris and Michael ever in the spotlight of her memory, she failed miserably. Did Michael love Chris? Was this talented and beautiful woman to be a permanent part of his future? And how could she, Laura—a newcomer to Michael's life— compete with Chris? Except for a few kisses, one moonlit night, Michael had maintained a discreet distance between them. If anything, he went out of his way to avoid Laura.

A soft knocking on her door interrupted Laura's restless thoughts. "Yes!" she called.

"It's me . . . Chris," came the answer.

Laura groaned inwardly. What did she want? To underscore her warning? Laura pulled open the door and forced a smile to her face. "Is there something I can do to help you?"

Chris looked at her curiously and said, "A man is here to see you. He's downstairs in the hotel conference room . . ."

Laura was genuinely surprised. *Who in the world?* She didn't know a soul other than Michael's people here in Bolivia. "Are you sure?" she asked Chris.

"He asked for Laura Garland," Chris shrugged. "I just happened to be near the desk when he came in.

112

He's an American," she added. "He's waiting in a small room off the lobby."

Laura was mystified, but she went down the hall, took the elevator to the lobby, then followed Chris to a door next to the manager's desk. The instant she opened the door, she felt her father's commanding presence.

"Mac!" she cried. He whirled to face her. He appeared tired, drawn; his color, pale. His massive shoulders sagged under his lightweight trenchcoat and he kept clenching his powerful hands into tight fists. His blue-eyed gaze sliced through her like cold-tempered steel.

"What is going on?" he asked, his voice barely audible.

Laura shrank against the door. Her heart pounded and her mouth went dry. Her surprise and momentary pleasure at seeing him evaporated into the staid, motionless air of the tiny room. She steeled herself and looked him squarely in the eye. "Whatever do you mean?" she asked coolly.

"I mean," he said with emphasis, "what do you think you're doing down here in Bolivia?"

"I telegraphed you when I arrived three days ago . . ." she said defensively, crossing to the far side of the room, away from him and the door. She reached up and pulled the chain to start the overhead fan turning.

"Monica said you packed your bags and left Cannes in the middle of the night. The next thing I know you're in this God-forsaken country . . ." his voice rose in pitch.

"It's hardly 'God-forsaken'." The voice was Michael's. He came into the room, shutting the door behind him. He wore a look of thunder on his face and his eyes never left Mac Garland's.

"You!" Mac fairly spat the word at Michael. "What have you done to my daughter?" He swiftly

113

walked to Michael and glowered into the younger man's eyes.

Laura held her breath. She was frightened. She'd never seen either man angry, truly angry, before. It was a fearsome sight. Like watching two predators circling each other before the kill.

"Mac!" Laura cried, putting herself physically between them.

"Actually," Michael continued, as if she'd never spoken, "the Spirit of God is alive and well in Bolivia. He's not forsaken anything or anyone here." His words were an indictment of Mac's world and they all knew it.

"Raintree . . ." Mac said through clenched teeth. "This is a private conversation between me and my daughter. Now get out!"

Michael didn't flinch, and made no move to leave.

Mac glared at Laura and barked, "I'm taking you home. Go pack!"

She stared at him, her mouth agape. He had ordered her about as if she were a child!

Her own temper flared. "I'm not going anywhere, Mac!" she exclaimed.

"Oh, yes, you are!" Mac shot back. He reached out, as if to grab her.

Michael's hand caught his in a steel grip. "If Laura wants to leave," he said quietly, "she can leave under her own power."

Mac flashed Michael a dark and livid look. He struggled for words, but seemed unable to find them. Pulling free of Michael's hold, he demanded, "All right, Laura. If you won't come home with me, then go back to Cannes. After all, there's someone there who really loves you . . . Brad told me . . ."

She shot him a look that stopped his words short. Suddenly, she understood why Brad had turned up in Cannes. "You sent him, didn't you?" Her voice was low and accusing. "You sent Brad to keep an eye on me, to wine and dine me, to . . . to . . ." Her voice rose and shook with indignation.

"You could do a lot worse than Brad!" Mac snapped defensively, a red flush coming over his face as he realized his manipulations had been discovered.

"Really?" Laura shot back. "Well, someday, Mac, I'll tell you what your meddling almost cost me!"

Mac stared at her for a long moment. Then he brushed aside her comment. "Are you coming home with me now?"

Laura felt something rise up within her—a resolve, an inner strength, a determination. "No," she said softly. "I'm not going, Mac. I'm staying."

Mac stared open-mouthed at her. He struggled to speak, fumed silently, then at last dismissed her statement and directed his next question to Michael. "What have you done to her? What kind of brainwashing have you used on her?"

"I've done nothing to her," Michael said quietly. "Laura's a grown woman. She's made her own decision."

Laura glanced up at him, grateful for his words. She found compassion in his blue eyes. And a deep, untapped source of strength and comfort for her battered heart. She loved them both—both of these proud stubborn men—but she knew what she had to do.

"Have you, Laura? Made your decision?" Mac asked. His voice had once again grown hard and cold.

"Yes, Mac . . ." she restated. "I'm staying."

He took a deep breath, pursed his lips, and thrust his hands deep into his coat pockets. Then he took a different tack. "All right, Raintree. How much?" he asked, glancing past his daughter into Michael's face.

"What?" Michael asked, leaning forward as if he hadn't quite understood.

"I asked, 'How much?'" Mac repeated with ruthless cunning. "How much will it take for you to

115

leave my daughter alone? I can set up a numbered account for you in Switzerland. You can do a lot of 'ministry' with that kind of money. Name your price.''

For a moment the room grew deathly quiet. Nothing stirred. No one spoke. Even the overhead fan seemed to stop spinning. Michael's eyes blazed with a cold fire. "I've already been bought and paid for, Mr. Garland,'' Michael said with immense control. "It was a blood offering!"

As the full impact of Michael's words hit him, Mac's face turned livid with rage. His hands trembled and he could hardly catch his breath. For a moment, Laura feared for her father's life.

The huge man pulled himself up to his full height and glared from Michael to Laura and back to Michael again. "Very well," he hissed viciously. "Then stay, Laura. Stay and play your games. But I'm telling you . . . you will never see a dime of my money. As of this moment . . . you are forever out of my will and out of my life!" He strode to the door and jerked it open, where he turned and lashed out with one final statement. "I'll give your best to your mother!"

He walked out the door, past the startled desk clerk, and through the lobby. Laura watched him go in stunned silence. For all his haughty and hurtful words, she saw an almost imperceptible droop to his shoulders and an uneasiness in his step. Suddenly, Mackenzie Garland looked like a beaten man. And, somehow . . . very old.

116

## CHAPTER 8

AFTER LAURA WATCHED HER FATHER step outside into the bright Bolivian afternoon, she quietly closed the door, then stood and stared at its hard, dark surface. She felt numb and empty inside. It was a full minute before she realized that Michael was still in the room with her.

She turned to face him. When she opened her mouth to speak, no words came out. He reached for her and suddenly, Laura found herself in the warm, protective circle of his arms. She buried her face against his broad, firm chest. Then she wept.

Great, racking sobs, deep and anguished, from the recesses of her heart, poured out of her. She had broken with her past, yet she did not know her future. She teetered emotionally on the brink of the unknown, clinging to Michael while her tears saturated the front of his shirt.

Somehow he slipped her a handkerchief and she muffled her tears with it. He stood holding her for a long time, until her river of grief had subsided.

Michael rocked her gently in his arms, resting his

chin atop her head. Finally, when she was entirely spent, he drew back and looked down at her bowed head.

"All right now?" he asked softly.

She raised her red-rimmed eyes to his and nodded, unable to trust her voice.

Michael cradled her face tenderly in his hands, running his thumbs under her eyes to smooth away the dampness. His voice sounded low and husky as he asked hesitantly, "This Brad . . . did he . . . did he hurt you?"

Laura shook her head, drawn by something deep within his violet-blue eyes—something more than concern or curiosity. And she felt a stirring within herself—a quiet longing to dissolve into him, to meld with his flesh . . . to belong to him. Gently and very slowly, he brought his mouth down on hers. His kiss was soft and warm, filled with a sweetness that shook her to the core of her being.

She pulled away at last, trembling, her emotions so frayed and battered that she couldn't think straight. Her life had fallen down around her. She had nowhere to go. Michael was the only person left who had a place for her. But he didn't need her complicating his life. He'd told her so long ago.

And she didn't want his pity—couldn't stand the thought of his feeling sorry for her, or of letting her stay because he felt "responsible" for her. She backed slowly toward the door, her eyes riveted on his, like a stricken animal caught in a cruel steel-jawed trap. No, Michael's pity was the one thing she couldn't live with. She loved him far too much.

The door handle jabbed her in the small of her back. She reached behind her, turned the knob, and backed out the doorway. Then she turned and crossed quickly to the elevator. Once its doors closed behind her, she leaned against the cool, steel surface. There were no tears left.

Alone in her room, Laura weighed her options. She

could return home. Mac would forgive her if she went home immediately. He'd write her a check, give her a job, and smooth out the wrinkles of her recent rebellion. Laura shuddered, her mind recoiling at the prospect of that solution. Or she could stay in Bolivia. She wanted to remain with Michael. She wanted to work with his ministry. She wanted to be of value to the kingdom of God.

Laura washed her face and reapplied her make-up, in order to keep her hands busy and have something to do by rote—to concentrate on "doing" and not on "feeling."

A soft knock on her door snapped her from her bleak thoughts. "Who is it?" she called, not wanting to see anyone.

"It's me . . . Michael."

She took a deep breath and opened her door to him. He was standing in the hallway, an ancient typewriter in his hands. "Thought you might need this if you're going to be doing a newsletter for the States," he told her.

Her eyes flew to his face. She saw only kindness and determination written on his features. Her heart flooded with gratitude and renewed commitment. He was right. Life must go on. She had made promises to both God and Michael. A new path for her life had been charted and she couldn't be sidetracked by old loyalties.

"Come in," Laura said hastily. "Put it over there." She indicated a small table in her hotel room.

Michael set down the ancient machine. "I have some notes you'll need in order to get started."

Laura stared at the contraption for a moment. "Hmm," she mused, "where's the plug?"

Michael threw back his head and laughed. His eyes twinkled. "Some of the greatest writers in the world got their start on machines like this. Consider this your golden opportunity to recapture the days of Hemingway, Faulkner, Fitzgerald . . ."

". . . broken fingernails, frustration, and messy ribbons," she finished with a mock sigh.

"Look," Michael said. "I have an idea . . . I'm not preaching until tomorrow night. Have you seen much of La Paz?"

"Only on the way here from the airport," she said.

"It's a terrific afternoon. Come with me. I'll show you some of the more famous places in the city. We'll have dinner down in the city plaza. We could take off right now. What do you say?"

Her heart leaped with anticipation. An entire afternoon and evening with Michael! "I'd like that very much," she said quietly. "And, Michael, " she added, "thank you. Thank you for understanding."

He offered her a lopsided grin and then guided her out of the room. Together they made their way out of the hotel into the crisp, cool, bright air of La Paz—the City of Peace.

Michael brought her into the heart of the city, to a grassy promenade called the Sixteenth of July Street. In the Plaza Venezuela they entered the San Francisco Church and monastery, old and intricately beautiful with its high Renaissance arches, its great high altar ablaze with candle fire and reverberating with the echoes of time.

"How beautiful . . ." Laura whispered.

"Yet how lonely," Michael commented beside her. "I felt this way in Europe, too, when I visited one of those great cathedrals. It's as if the Spirit of God had moved out. As if these mausoleums had become too 'holy' . . . too removed from the masses of people." Michael's voice grew heavy with conviction. "I believe that God lives in the hearts of his people. The real church is found within the body of His believers."

Laura only nodded. She understood what he meant. The great stone edifice was, indeed, beautiful. But she felt no sense of the presence of God there. At least, not in the same way as when she worshiped among the crowds of people at the Mission. There she felt the fervor of their hunger for God . . .

Back outside in the dazzling light of day, Laura and Michael strolled along the great Plaza in quiet contentment. He took her hand, engulfing it in his own, and she leaned into his side, feeling safe and protected. High above the city, in the distance, she focused dreamily on the snow-capped peaks of the Andes.

"I think I'm finally adjusting to the altitude," she said.

"It does take a few days," he assured her. His step quickened and his voice took on an adventurous tone when he suggested, "Come on. Let's go down to the marketplace. I'll bet you've never seen anything like it!"

The marketplace of La Paz teemed with mercantile activity. Booths, vendors, and makeshift stalls lined narrow walkways. Every square inch seemed to be covered with fruit, food, cloth, flowers, and animals. All of it was for sale.

Indian women and children with flat features worked the booths and stalls. The women, dressed in bowler hats, colorful, full dresses, twinkling silver earrings, and woolen ponchos, wore their black hair in broad plaits.

"These ladies are among the shrewdest merchants in the world," Michael told Laura. "Much of the economy of Bolivia rests on their shoulders."

Laura walked from booth to booth, wide-eyed. The array of merchandise was mind-boggling. She saw succulent fruits—peaches, bananas, mangoes, pears, quinces, guavas. She marveled at bright green and red parrots, sitting on makeshift perches, and atop cages of parakeets, toucans, and cockatoos. She saw piles of llama skins, soft and silky. There were ponchos of heavy wool, bolts of hand-loomed linen and cotton.

"I think I'll buy a poncho," she told Michael, running her hands over the pile of goods on one table.

So he bartered with the seller until both were satisfied that the price and the product were matched.

"I'd have paid twice as much," Laura admitted as she slipped the poncho over her head. The temperature was dropping in the waning sunlight, and the garment felt warm.

"But bartering is the way of life here," Michael explained. "They expect you to argue over the price."

"Where do all these people come from?" she asked.

"From all over Bolivia," he said. "From the Yungas, the valley lands; from the Oriente, the lowlands; and the Savannas, where they do a lot of farming and cattle ranching. La Paz is the city of dreams for much of the population."

Laura stopped abruptly in front of a booth lush with flowers and greenery. "Oh, Michael, look!" she cried. She picked up a flaming red flower, drooping with clusters of blossoms.

"That's the *kantuta* flower," he said. "Translated, it means 'the fountain of blood.' It's very beautiful, isn't it?"

"Oh, yes!" she marveled.

"It's yours," he told her and bought it from the vendor.

"Thank you. I've always loved flowers, and this one is extra special to me." It was true—of all the flowers she'd ever received as gifts, none was more precious than this wild, crimson cascade from the peaks of Bolivia. It had come from Michael.

She dropped her eyes quickly, lest he read her thoughts. "What's this?" she asked, fingering some small bunches of dried leaves.

"Coca leaves," Michael told her. "Chemically treated and powdered, it's known as cocaine."

"Out here?" she gasped in disbelief. "In the open?"

Michael laughed. "It's perfectly legal," he assured

122

her. "The Bolivians make a tea from these leaves which has a calming effect on the central nervous system. In fact, these mountain Indians get a daily ration of coca leaves. It makes their lives more livable," he added somewhat grimly. "The Incas discovered its medicinal properties centuries ago and the people still use it today. It's one of the things I hope to help them learn—that with a life in Christ, you don't need coca leaves to survive."

"Funny," Laura mused, recalling the world's war on cocaine, "how so much grief can be caused by such tiny little pieces of vegetation . . ."

"Such is the nature of sin," Michael grinned, acknowledging that she had perceived a simple truth about the ways of man. "Mankind has always had a knack for perverting God's provisions. Now, you'd better change the subject before I start preaching and attract a crowd."

"Then how about dinner?" Laura urged. "I'm starved!"

He took her to a small café-style restaurant, one of many that lined the Prado. She felt cozy indoors, snug in her woolen poncho.

"Enjoy the winter while you can," he told her.

"Winter? What do you mean?" she asked, glancing up from her menu.

"In several weeks, we'll be leaving La Paz for the interiors. In the lowlands, it's like Miami in the worst of summers—without air conditioning," he added.

Laura's heart beat more quickly. So his plans included her. She didn't care how miserable the weather might be, so long as she could be with Michael.

For dinner, he helped her choose a delicious Bolivian dish called *empanada saltena,* a crusty flour pastry filled with chopped meat, olives, raisins, potatoes, hot sauce, and peppers. Her mouth tingled exotically. She loved it!

Michael chose *picante de pollo,* a heaping serving

of fried chicken, fried potatoes, rice, and hot peppers. He offered her a taste and she liked that, too. They drank mineral water from thick, fluted glasses and shared a dessert of fried bananas.

With the meal completed, Michael hailed a cab and they returned to the hotel. At her room door, Laura told him, "Thank you. This day with you was the perfect prescription. I feel much better."

The dim lights of the hallway caused her to feel hushed and subdued, but when she gazed up into Michael's eyes she lost her emotional bearings, and almost offered her lips to him for a kiss.

Michael kept his hands at his sides. "Today was my pleasure," he said softly. "Now get some sleep. Doctor's orders," he joked. "Once you start on that newsletter tomorrow, you'll find I'm a regular tyrant to work for." Yet, the smile that played about his mouth belied his words.

Later, she lay in bed, mulling over the past few months of her life. So much had happened! So many things were different! She realized that although one door had closed in her life, God had allowed another to open for her. And now, here she was, light-years away from all the people, places, and things she had ever known. Strangely enough, she was at peace and filled with a sense of purpose and destiny.

There were still many unanswered questions— much to learn. Yet she knew that she was walking in the will of God. And that realization brought her an inner peace she had not known before—a feeling she realized now she had been searching for most of her life.

And she also knew that somehow her destiny was intertwined with that of Michael Raintree's. Somehow . . . someway . . .

The next few weeks were the busiest of Laura's life. She rewrote Michael's newsletter until he was completely satisfied with it. She worked with a local typesetter to get it camera-ready for printing. It was decided that the final stats, the finished ready-to-be-printed paste-ups, would be mailed to the States, where supporters of Michael's ministry would have it printed and distributed throughout the country.

Laura also began organizing and writing out Michael's messages and various notes for a series of teaching seminars he was planning in La Paz in the upcoming months. A young woman in Rey's church helped translate the information into Spanish for her before this material, too, was typeset and reproduced for mass distribution.

As the weeks passed, Michael held greatly successful crusades in larger and larger buildings in La Paz, reaching increasing numbers of people with his message. The power of his preaching stirred the city's political and social hierarchy, and his meetings began to attract people in positions of wealth, prominence, and authority.

Billy acted as Michael's emissary, setting up meeting places, dealing with myriad requests for his time and presence, acting as a general liaison with parties opposed to Michael's missionary influence over the population. The pressure and demands on both men were both physically and emotionally draining, but they worked with single-minded dedication.

During the fever-pitched pace of the next weeks, Laura was careful to keep her relationship with Michael on a professional level. She divided her thoughts and feelings into two separate compartments. One held her business skills and her commitment to provide the ministry with her business expertise. The other held her love for Michael, the man. While it was a tightrope act—balancing her analytical side with her emotional side—Laura managed. The end result was that it removed a lot of internal pressure and allowed her to work next to him without having her feelings interfering during their long hours together.

She continued to have an affinity for Lisa, finding her a kind and thoughtful friend. And although Laura and Chris formed an alliance born out of mutual goals and service to the ministry, Laura recognized an underlying coolness in Chris's treatment of her. However, she was far too busy to dwell on it. So she simply kept her distance from the woman, giving no offense, nor accepting any.

In August, Michael called a staff meeting to explain that it was time to move into the interiors of Bolivia. The rainy season would begin in October and November and continue through May. Travel to the smaller cities within the jungles and savannas would be greatly restricted.

"We'll go into Cochabamba first," he told the group. "Then on to Trinidad on the Mamore River, and finally, into Magdalena, where conditions are really primitive. We'll take a train to Cochabamba—it's about fourteen hours worth of beautiful scenery—" he added when everyone groaned. "Then a plane—and I use that term loosely—to Trinidad." He smiled. "Of course, we could wait for a cargo boat to take us up the river, if you don't mind a two-week journey."

Moans of protest ricocheted through the room.

"All right . . ." Michael laughed, gesturing with upraised palms. "Great explorers, you're not! Anyway, we'll fly into both Trinidad and Magdalena. I understand that one of the high points in a Magdalenian's week is the arrival of the airplane, bringing visitors . . ."

The important business of defining personal agendas, the amount of luggage each could take, what kind of clothes to pack, and other details replaced their good-natured complaints.

"In Magdalena, we'll be the guests of Theil Swensen. He's a missionary doctor from Norway," Michael explained. As he talked, Laura thought the plans exciting, intriguing. She looked forward to the travel and to meeting the Swensens. Michael continued, "Theil and his family have been living and ministering in the city for about fifteen years. He's very anxious to have us come. He's a great man of God and I want very much to work with him.

"Recently he's been getting a lot of pressure from the local politicos. They're becoming more and more vocal. It's time for revival—for God to be presented as a choice for the people."

The room grew quiet as they considered Michael's words. He was right. None of them could afford to forget why they were in Bolivia. The battle was real. It was a battle for the souls of men. Laura took a deep breath and, after the meeting broke up, she went thoughtfully back to her room. That night, she prayed for God's guidance and protection over their journey.

The train to Cochabamba was an ancient contraption, rattling and puffing with tremendous effort up, out of the valley of La Paz, and down through the treacherous mountain passes into the mid-lands of Bolivia—the Yungas.

Michael's group consisted of the Sonshine Singers, Billy, Laura, and a young Bolivian, Enrique Chavez, who was a college student at the *Universidad Mayor de San Andres* in La Paz, and a member of Rey's church. One day Enrique hoped to become a minister himself. He would act as translator for Michael's meetings, since he was fluent in Spanish, Quechuan and Aymaran, the three principal languages spoken in the country.

Laura liked Enrique, a dark-eyed man with a soft voice, thick straight black hair and facial features that bespoke his Spanish-Indian ancestry. She sat next to him on the twisting train ride into Cochabamba, as he pointed out various sights and recited bits of local history. She learned that the Spaniards had come to

Bolivia in the fourteenth century, searching for riches, subduing the great Inca empire, and influencing the country for centuries to follow.

Once the train passed through the mountains, Laura saw the deep blue haze of vast forests below and smelled the new scent of moist, rich earth in the rapidly warming, humid air. As the vehicle chugged through the thickening jungles, she grew fascinated by the rich variety of plants and trees.

Enrique pointed out mahogany, walnut, jacaranda, special types of palms . . . a forest of untapped resources. Occasionally, when the train slowed, she saw groups of monkeys, leaping from tree to tree, squawking and screeching above the noise of the train.

When at last they reached Cochabamba, a big, sprawling city, they were bone-weary, after almost two days of constant vibration from the train. Laura fell asleep instantly in her hotel room, missing supper and not waking until early the next morning.

The crusade began that night, in the city's largest soccer stadium. Thousands of people came to hear Michael preach, and, as he walked to the platform in the center of the arena, Laura felt awed reverence for the God who had blessed her so richly by allowing her to be a part of His master plan.

They remained in the city one week. Michael preached, counseled, and met with area ministers, spreading the fire of the gospel to the far ends of the region with his revival. Laura found herself acting as liaison and spokesperson with the press. She felt comfortable with the job, realizing the importance of accurate representation for Michael's ministry. The news media still tended to focus on the man and his incredible charisma and not always on his gospel message.

At the end of the week, they left Cochabamba for Trinidad, a city set deeper in the jungle interiors, not as large and not as modernized. "You could only get here by river at one time," Enrique told Laura once they got off the plane. "Now, at least, there's a faster way."

The air in Trinidad was even more humid, reminding her of Miami in the grip of summer. But the people who attended Michael's meetings were just as eager, just as hungry for the message he had for them. The Singers were well received by the music-loving Bolivians. And even though they couldn't understand the words, they took joy in the rhythm of the music, the beauty of Chris's voice, the blend of the harmonies.

Laura discovered that she was truly enjoying herself. The work was demanding, yet she found it fulfilling, in a way she'd never known selling real estate. She found to her surprise that she had even developed a compassion for these people. She no longer felt awkward and ill-at-ease around them as she once had felt at the Mission back in Miami. Sometimes, she even felt a part of them, a kinship born of belonging to and serving in the same kingdom . . . the kingdom of God.

She never stopped being fascinated by Michael's spiritual maturity and by his ability to summon exactly the right words for every group. By his command of biblical knowledge. Nor ceased to be amazed by his power and authority over the unseen forces that came against him in the form of political pressure, government apathy and the sheer numbers of people who struggled to touch him, have him pray for them, minister to them.

The last night they were in Trinidad, they went to the far outskirts of the town, where some of the poorest inhabitants lived in thatched-roofed houses of mud and wattle. The evangelistic team arrived as special and honored guests, with the entire neighborhood turning out to greet them. In a central meeting hall, they ate food that had been cooked on an open fire by peasant women, encumbered with numerous wide-eyed, dirty-faced children.

Laura ate cautiously, not really sure what she was eating. She noticed Chris and Lisa also picking at their food—wide, flat flour bread; *locro,* a soupy rice dish, seasoned with salt and lard and filled with bananas and yucca; followed by mangoes and nuts for dessert.

"Vegetables are practically unheard of," Enrique told her across the wobbly table they shared. "Since civilization has arrived here, the people have discovered candy. They'd live on a diet of candy and potatoes if they could. They're lucky to get meat twice a week."

The air in the room was hot and oppressive. Laura grew restless. She noticed Michael in deep conversation with two local Bolivian ministers; Billy, counseling a man in another part of the room, while Lisa, Chris, Jack and Phil sang light songs for the children, who flocked around them in fascination.

One child, a boy about four, reached out timidly and touched Chris's silken hair. "*Oro* . . ." he mumbled. "Gold," Enrique translated.

Chris picked him up and set him on her lap, smiling into his huge black eyes. He sat rigid, staring at her face, musing aloud in Spanish that she must be an angel.

Suddenly Laura could not endure the confinement a second longer. She rose and went outside into the night, to pace the village compound. She felt oddly disjointed, unsettled. She thought back to that first time she'd heard Michael in Biscayne Park, in Miami. How different her life had become since that day! How alien to all she'd ever known before. She wondered about her parents. Mac and Ellen . . . what were they doing this night? And Monica . . . where was she now?

She stood on the edge of the village, leaning against a smooth-barked tree, staring into the inky blackness of the Bolivian night and felt a pang of homesickness wash over her.

"Laura . . ." Michael said her name, and she spun with a start, adrenalin pumping through her body.

"Oh!" she gasped. "Y-you frightened me . . ."

"I'm sorry," he said, stepping in front of her. "But when I looked up, you were gone, and I was concerned. I thought I'd better come find you. This is the jungle, after all. It's not a very safe place to be alone at night . . ."

His nearness calmed her. "You know," she whispered thoughtfully, "I never knew the night could be so dark. Where we live, artificial lights take away the darkness. Until now, I didn't know what night was really like . . ."

He moved toward her protectively and she tensed, torn between wanting him to touch her and fearing that he would not. She worked so hard to erect a wall around her feelings for him.

'I-I was just thinking . . ." She felt his arm slide around her shoulders—"Out here, my father's name . . . his money, his influence . . . it counts for nothing . . ."

"Laura," Michael said, his voice soft and low, "Out here your *real* Father's name counts for everything."

They stood together silently, each reflecting on inner thoughts, when the sound of a distant scream floated through the darkness, causing the hair to stand up on her arms. "What was *that?*" she asked in a hushed whisper.

"Jaguar," he told her matter-of-factly. "The jungles are full of them."

She felt a playful smile on her lips. "Funny," she whispered teasingly, "It didn't *sound* like a sports car . . ."

Michael laughed aloud, the sound deep and throaty. He hugged her warmly and said, "It's all in your frame of reference, I guess. Actually, jaguars are pretty interesting beasts." His voice grew serious. "They're one of the few animals who will hunt man.

131

That's why they're so dangerous. Most animals will run from us. But those cats will turn on you. Often, the hunter becomes the hunted."

She shuddered as the great cat screamed again, his cry melting into the jungle. Michael stepped behind her; his hands rested lightly on her shoulders. "You're tense." Gently he began to rub her neck and shoulders.

A shiver shot up her spine. She could feel her carefully constructed shield of indifference beginning to crumble. She was aware of every breath he took, every move he made. *Walk away*, she commanded herself. But she couldn't.

A brilliant flash of insight swept over her then. And she realized that in another life, before he'd ever known God, Michael Raintree had known women— known them intimately—their nature, their needs, their weaknesses.

Surely it was his special curse, his thorn in the flesh, to be so incredibly handsome, so filled with a passion for life and so burdened with the weight of his own desires, the sum of his very nature.

It was an ironic judgment of God, she thought. To be fueled by one's passions, yet be a slave to them. Chris's words came back to her—words spoken prophetically, in what seemed a lifetime ago: "Many women have been attracted to Michael the man and have used his message as a pretense to get close to him."

It would have been that way for Laura, too . . . if God had not pricked her conscience. Or if Michael had been less a man of God and more a man of the world. In her former life, she would have given herself to him gladly. But he had wisely kept his distance, either not recognizing her simmering love for him or refusing to succumb to a relationship that would forever change the complexion of their higher callings. Yet right now, in the soft dark arms of shadow, Laura felt her resolve wavering.

*Michael! Michael!* Her heart hammered his name, and a wind tinged with fire swept through her. He turned her slowly around, his hands gripping her upper arms with impassioned purpose. She couldn't see his face. The night was too dark. But she sensed that it was inches from her own. Dangerous inches.

*If I kiss him now,* she told herself through the fog of her own hunger, *there will be no turning back.* She couldn't take that road—not for her sake, not for Michael's. Slowly, as if in a dream, she pulled back, away from the luscious descent of his lips. If they touched, she would be pulled into a vortex of passion from which she could not break free. A tempest of self-destruction which would forever mark them both.

Her heart felt as if it might explode from her breast. But she slid from beneath his hold and stepped backwards, her heel snapping a branch.

"It's late . . ." she said hoarsely.

"Yes . . ." Michael agreed, his voice quiet and all but shaking with the realization of what had almost happened between them.

He took her arm, grasping her hand tightly and fairly pulled her back toward the Bolivian village. Away from the concealing canopy of night. Back toward the warmth of the open firelights . . .

## CHAPTER 9

THEY DID NOT SPEAK of that night again. And even in the bright light of day, Laura could find no trace of the intense, seething desire in Michael's eyes when they met with the rest of the group at the airfield for the flight to Magdalena. But she felt as if she had been tested . . . as metal by fire . . . and that she had survived the furnace.

The plane that took the group to Magdalena was World War II vintage, with propellers. Long metal benches lined both sides of the interior of the plane and thirty people crowded onto them, scrunched together, elbow to elbow. All luggage and personal belongings were heaped in the center of the plane's metal flooring. Laura hoped they hit no pockets of bad weather. Nothing was secured, and turbulence could prove both uncomfortable and dangerous.

The plane was more than three hours late in leaving Trinidad, but she had come to accept this delay as the way of Bolivians. They were people with little regard for schedules.

By the time they landed in the city of Magdalena,

on the fringes of the jungle, Laura felt as if she were tied in knots. She was hot, tired, cramped, and claustrophobic. She longed to stand up and stretch her legs and breathe in fresh air. They disembarked the old silver aircraft and were met by a throng of locals who seemed overjoyed with their arrival. A man approached their small group from the fringes of the crowd.

"Michael!" the man called, embracing the taller, younger man.

"Theil . . ." Michael returned.

Laura appraised Theil Swensen. He was rail-thin, about six feet tall, sixtyish, with a full head of pure white hair, light blue eyes, and a tanned face that spoke volumes of a harsh life in the sun. Yet he had an authoritative air, a smile that enlivened his entire presence and a firm, crisp voice with only the trace of a Nordic accent.

After introductions, Theil led them all to his Jeep and after three trips, hauling people and luggage, Laura found herself on a dirt road, in front of a run-down building that Theil referred to as the "Magdalena Arms." There was a definite note of sarcasm in his voice. Then he added, "It isn't the Hilton, but it will do. Besides," he added, "it's the only place in town."

Laura viewed it with dismay. The façade was worn, run-down and badly in need of paint. A cluster of chickens squawked from the center of the road as a boy tried to hurry them out of the way of an oxdrawn cart.

"Look," Theil continued, "I must get back to the clinic. Get settled in and I'll pick you up for dinner tonight at my house. Helga has been cooking for a week. We're glad you're here, Michael. There's much we need to discuss," he finished in a more somber tone.

After Theil left them, Michael arranged for rooms for everyone. The hotel was small, much like an inn.

135

Each earthen-floored room contained two cots and a dresser. A window overlooked the dirt street. With a sinking feeling, Laura realized that she would not be able to have her own private room. Like it or not, she would be rooming with Chris.

The two women put away their belongings in awkward silence. Laura took the bottom two drawers of the dresser and then laid out her overnight case and her hairbrush in the cubbyhole of a bathroom. The shower stall was ancient, with peeling paint streaked with hard-water stains. She sighed and went back into the room, sitting down heavily on one of the narrow cots. The mattress felt no thicker than the depth of a wadded towel.

The room was unbearably hot, the air thick and stuffy. She found a piece of paper in her purse and fanned the perspiration from her neck and face. Chris sat in the room's lone chair, combing the fine-spun silver of her hair. "Bet these accommodations are a far cry from anything you're used to."

Laura bristled. "Different decorator," she ventured sourly. She felt too tired and hot to spar with Chris verbally.

Chris refused to be put off. "Do you ever hear from your father?"

Her tone was casual, but Laura felt the barb. Her last encounter with Mac festered within her like an open wound. "Why do you ask?"

Chris leveled her saucer-shaped blue eyes at Laura's green-eyed look of defiance and said innocently, "He came after you—all the way to Bolivia . . ." She shrugged and began to weave her hair into a long braid. "It seems such a shame to be alienated so totally from one's family."

Laura's temper flared and she bounded off the bed. "You couldn't possibly understand the complexity of Mac's and my relationship!" she snapped, crossing to the window. Laura stared out into the dusty street, struggling to regain control of her temper, feeling as if Chris had jerked the dressing off the wound and left it exposed and throbbing. Outside, partially-clothed children played freely, squealing and running. A thin spiral of smoke rose from an open cooking fire and peasant women stirred pots of soup.

"You think I don't understand?" Chris challenged softly from her perch across the room.

Laura surveyed her again, biting back her words, watching as Chris's fingers laced her hair into a shining rope.

"Maybe I don't, to your way of thinking," Chris fired hotly. "But by the time I was twelve I'd been in so many foster homes I'd lost count. I never saw my father's face, Laura. Never even knew his name. I don't know what it's like to have a father who cares enough to follow me halfway around the world. I was merely curious as to why you'd throw that kind of relationship aside without making some effort to redeem it!"

Laura's cheeks burned. She felt both chastised and humbled. Chris had not been looking for a fight, yet Laura had offered her one. She felt a prickling sensation in her eyes and averted her face quickly. "I'm sorry," she said. "I had no idea . . ."

"It isn't important," Chris said, rising from the bed and securing her hair with a golden clip. "I think I'll go for a walk before we go to the Swensens' tonight." She picked up her Bible and added, "I'll find a place to do some reading while it's still light. I heard Billy say that the town generator only produces electricity from six until midnight." She tugged on her sandals and left the bleak room quickly.

Laura admonished herself once she was alone. "Fool!" For the first time Chris had made an overture of friendliness. And Laura had blown it. "Forgive me, Lord," she asked aloud and promised not to destroy the opportunity should it ever arise again. The news

137

about the generator also unsettled her. How could an entire town exist without electricity? How could the Swensens live with only six hours of electricity a day? It wasn't easy, Laura decided grimly. It wasn't easy living this life Michael lived.

Fiercely she raked a comb through her hair and glared at her image in the cracked mirror over the dresser. "I'm no quitter!" she told herself. "God wants me here. I just know it!"

From the outside the Swensen home was like many others in the town. But inside, the similarity ended. The rooms were filled with subtle little touches of the Swensens' homeland. An ornate dining table, a white lace cloth, and an assortment of colorful candles decorated the dining room.

The rich, delicate aroma of roasting chicken, fresh dark bread, and baking potatoes filled the small house. Helga Swensen was a big woman with light brown hair, blue eyes, and large, rough, reddened hands. She was intelligent and soft-spoken and doted on her husband. She was also a nurse and worked long hours beside him in their clinic. Laura admired the older woman's spirit and seemingly endless energy and dedication.

The visitors clustered around the table with Theil and Helga, laughing and talking, enjoying each other's company along with heaping plates of the delicious homecooked food. Michael shared news from the States and told of his work thus far in Bolivia. Theil listened attentively, nodding and asking occasional questions.

Theil leaned back in his chair and appraised Michael. Finally, he asked, "How long has it been, Michael? How long since we met?"

Michael smiled, an inward smile that played about the corners of his sensuous mouth and caused Laura to look away, jealous of his existence before she knew him. "Ten years?" Michael ventured.

"I first saw this young man back in the States at a conference in Texas," Theil reminisced. "I was attending a Bible seminar . . . there were missionaries, ministers, Bible teachers . . . you name it. A real collection of scholars and believers. Men who'd heard it all before, seen it all." Theil's eyes glowed as he spoke.

"Plus, I was raising money for the clinic back here in Bolivia on my own speaking tour. I never go to those seminars any more. No time," Theil laughed. "I was sitting there in this huge auditorium, thinking how bored I was and how much I missed my Helga . . ." He glanced over at his wife, who pursed her lips and smiled at him lovingly. ". . . and my work," he added.

"Then the chairman introduced this man," he nodded toward Michael. "And Michael strode out to the podium. So tall . . . so young . . . so confident. Just his presence alone caused everyone to look up, sit a little straighter in their seats, lean forward." Theil's eyes glistened with the memory.

"When he began his message, I knew at once that this was no ordinary speaker. This was a man on fire for God. Filled with the Spirit. Alive, intense, dedicated . . ."

Michael spoke. "Theil . . . come on now . . ."

"It's true!" Theil insisted. "When anyone can make a room full of tired old preachers and bored old men sit up and take note—well, then it's no accident." He paused. "It's God!" he added emphatically.

Laura could well imagine how Michael must have affected the group. She'd seen it too often herself. She'd felt the power of his love for God; known the convicting impact of his words, his voice, his message. Through Michael Raintree, she'd met God and seen her own nature as it really *was*.

"When I heard that you were in La Paz," Theil

continued, "I told Helga, 'This is a man who must come and speak to our people. God uses this man. We need him.' Did I not say this, Helga?"

Helga nodded. " *Ja*," she said. "He insisted that I contact Rey Ortiz by ham radio the very day we heard."

"The radio is our only way to contact the outside world," Theil explained to them. "Our daughter Inga keeps in touch with us by radio. She's in San Ramon, setting up a clinic for the farmers there."

"San Ramon?" Billy asked. "Isn't that in the South? In the savannas?"

"*Ja*," Helga said. "Very primitive! She works very hard. Every so often, whenever we can get away, we fly down in our plane to take her medical supplies, Bibles, whatever we have to share."

"You have a plane?" Michael asked.

"Just a small one," Theil told him. "A necessity— for medical emergencies, supply runs to Santa Cruz. I keep it in flying shape myself."

Laura marveled. A missionary, a doctor, a pilot-mechanic, a father . . . How much Theil gave to spread the gospel of Jesus Christ!

"Michael has a pilot's license," Chris mentioned casually.

"You do?" Theil's surveyed Michael with renewed interest. So did Laura.

"I've had one for years," Michael confirmed. "I like to go up every now and again . . . just for the fun of it."

Laura mused over the information. She remembered how much he'd loved driving her car. The natural and confident way he had commanded the vehicle. Again, she wondered what he would have been like if God had not intervened and directed him down another path.

"I want to talk to you more about that later," Theil said. "But first, I need to discuss your visit here. And your ministry to the people of Magdalena. They need to hear what you have to say, but, I fear there are some problems . . ." his voice trailed and Michael leaned forward expectantly.

"What do you mean?"

"Political pressure groups," Theil said flatly. "They have been agitating the people. Telling them lies about me, the clinic, the church . . ."

Laura felt her heart beat faster. *Political factions?* It all sounded so foreign and, in a way, frightening.

"Tell me about it," Michael said grimly.

"The local people, the residents . . . they lack education, discernment. They are easily influenced. Like children," Theil shook his head of white hair sadly. "An agitator, an outsider, Jorge Sanchez, has come here. He is not an ignorant man." Theil's eyes grew angry. "He has been well trained, well indoctrinated. He influences the people. He urges them to vote for men he can control. The goal is to dominate the government of Bolivia, of course. Jorge is an evil man . . . an evil influence."

The room grew quiet. They felt the impact of Theil's words and understood the implication of danger. "He holds rallies in the sports stadium where you will be speaking," Theil continued. "Every evening this week is booked to spread his propaganda and lies. I only tell you this, Michael, because you must know what you're up against."

A bright fire danced in Michael's eyes. "One crowd, one stadium . . ." he said softly. "Good!" he added firmly. "A fight. I love a good fight."

"Sanchez is a powerful foe," Theil warned.

"So am I," Michael told him. "But God's on my side. And therein lies the difference!"

A slow smile spread across Theil's worried face. His once-tired eyes glowed brightly. "I know that," he said. "That's why I asked you to come."

141

Michael returned the man's smile. "And that, my friend, is exactly why I'm here!"

Michael's men worked feverishly to get everything set up before the crowds arrived. The musicians plugged in their speakers, tested their equipment, arranged their material. Billy and Enrique conferred quietly in a corner. Laura twisted her hands nervously, trying hard to concentrate on her note-taking for the news article she was preparing. There was an air of expectancy, a current of anticipation in the humid early evening light.

Michael had upstaged Jorge Sanchez. He'd arranged to start his gospel crusade a half hour earlier than Sanchez's meeting. Michael had booked the stadium right out from under the man for the entire week.

Laura saw him first—a small man, dark and swarthy, with cold soulless eyes and thin, cruel lips. He stood in the back of the stadium, watching the activity. Finally, he strode forward. He stopped directly in front of Laura, appraising her crudely. "What's the meaning of this?"

Her skin crawled, but she lifted her chin defiantly. "Our meeting begins in forty-five minutes. Why don't you come back then?"

"Who's in charge?" he demanded.

Before she could answer, Michael was standing beside her, towering over them with his presence and his strength.

"I'm in charge," he said. "I'm Michael Raintree. And you?"

"Jorge Sanchez," the man said. "What do you think you are doing?" he added in clipped, but fluent English.

"I'm holding a crusade for Christ," Michael explained with finality.

"But I have booked this stadium for a political

142

rally," Jorge shot back, refusing to be put off by Michael. "I've had it booked for weeks."

"When I'm finished, you may have it," Michael told him.

"When you're finished!" Jorge exploded. "Why, your rally could go on for hours! It will be too late for the people to stay for mine!"

"If your followers are no more loyal than that, Mr. Sanchez," Michael said smoothly, "then I would suggest that you examine the content of your message."

A vein pulsed in the side of Jorge's temple. He clenched and unclenched his fists. Laura drew back instinctively, touching the protective shield of Michael's chest.

"You are no holy man!" Jorge spat contemptuously.

"I never claimed to be holy," Michael said, leveling his searing blue eyes into Jorge's. "But the One I represent is holy. Whom do you represent, Mr. Sanchez? And how holy is he? Now, if you will excuse us . . ." He took Laura by her arm and stepped backward.

Jorge stared hatefully at them, powerless to change things. "You win this round, Mr. Raintree," he nodded coldly. "But there will be others . . ." The threat in his voice was real.

"No doubt," Michael affirmed. Together, they watched Jorge Sanchez stalk out of the stadium. A shiver ran through Laura. He reminded her of a hungry animal, content to wait and circle his prey, like one of the Bolivian jaguars Michael had warned her about. His words came back in a rush: " '. . . the hunter often becomes the hunted . . .' "

The crusade began and people poured in, lifting their voices and their hearts in praise. Laura found it hard to believe that such impassioned people could ever be influenced by the likes of Jorge Sanchez. The brilliance of Michael's message shone like a beacon of light. The simplicity of God's truth glowed like a solitary flame. Once again, Laura felt herself swept up into a higher place.

And she suddenly felt an all-encompassing love for these people—so trusting, so dependent. She remembered what Christ had said about entering the kingdom of God as a child and she understood completely how it could be possible. Michael had shown them a better world—a place of strength—a way to live so that their poverty did not destroy them. Jorge Sanchez and what he stood for did not have a chance as long as the people lived for Christ. She knew, too, that she had been as poor as they—despite all her money. She'd been poor and hungry and lonely. She watched Michael touch the people who listened eagerly, enraptured, absorbed with his words. Laura loved the people. She loved the man who enflamed them. And the God who held them all in His arms. And her love for Michael only grew stronger.

Long after midnight Laura lay awake, tossing and turning in the comfortless bed. The room was dark, the air still. She longed to get up and turn on a light and read. But there was no electricity. Besides, she didn't want to disturb Chris in the bed next to hers.

She exhaled deeply and tried counting backwards, concentrating on a long boring string of numbers, hoping that she would drift into sleep.

"You awake?" Chris asked softly into the darkened room.

"Yes," Laura confirmed. "Sorry if I disturbed you. . ."

"I can't sleep, either . . ."

Laura felt awkward, remembering their earlier conversation. She imagined Chris as a child, lonely, unwanted, being shuffled from foster home to foster home. She longed to talk to this woman. But she

144

didn't quite know what to say. Where to begin. Finally, Laura ventured, "It was a powerful meeting tonight, wasn't it?"

"Yes." Silence.

"I thought you singers were particularly good," Laura tried again. "You could be professionals, you know."

"We were."

Laura was surprised. She'd never really thought of their having careers prior to Michael's ministry. "When?" she asked, interested to know more about them.

"Back in Los Angeles. We had a rock group."

"How did you ever meet Michael?"

"We were doing a rock concert. One of those weekender things . . . fifty groups . . . thousands of screaming fans . . ." Chris painted a verbal picture of the past. "We were wiped out, heading no place . . . Lisa had joined the group mostly to keep her eye on Jack. He and Phil were into drugs . . ."

Laura listened intently, trying to imagine the friendly, outgoing Jack and the big, gentle Phil as longhaired freaks. She couldn't.

"Anyway . . ." Chris continued, "we had just finished our bit on stage. We were packing up our gear, trying hard to decide what to do next. The promoter had skipped . . . we didn't have the price of a meal between us. We looked up and there stood Billy Powell and Michael, staring at us . . ." Her voice began to pick up with excitement, recalling the encounter. "Michael said, 'You're very good. Why do you waste yourselves on that garbage?'"

Chris let out a low laugh. "Jack gave him a dirty scowl and asked, 'You got a gig for us, man?'"

Chris paused, then resumed quietly. "He started sharing Jesus with us, telling us things we had never heard before. Well . . . you know how Michael is . . . The next thing we knew we were on our knees, weeping, repenting, dedicating ourselves to Jesus.'' Chris stopped talking and Laura waited in the darkness, feeling the wonder of the group's experience.

Chris continued, her voice falling in waves of devotion. "We've been playing gospel music ever since. And following Michael wherever the Lord takes him. And we always will . . .'' she tacked on, as if in warning, in a tone that reconstructed the barrier between herself and Laura.

Once again Laura felt like an outsider. Chris had been here first. She'd known Michael longer. She'd loved him from the beginning . . . She, Laura, was the intruder.

"Thanks for telling me,'' Laura whispered into the stillness of the room, wishing somehow she could penetrate Chris's shield.

But Chris said nothing. The darkness hung between them like a curtain . . .


"Come this way, Michael, Laura. I want you to meet somebody . . .'' The two of them followed Theil through the row of beds in his clinic toward an area partitioned off by pale green drapes. The sharp smell of antiseptic permeated the brightly lit rectangular room.

Theil drew back the drapes. Laura saw a child lying on an expanse of crisp white sheets, an oxygen mask over her mouth and nose. Her hair was thick and black, her eyes dark and wide. Yet, in spite of her deep olive complexion, Laura could see an underlying bluish cast over her face and arms.

"This is Mara.'' Theil beamed down at the little girl. "Mara is twelve years old. I delivered her myself!''

Mara smiled shyly at them, her breath coming in labored gasps.

"Hello, Mara," Laura said softly, reaching out to touch the child's hand.

Mara's eyes grew wide as she stared at Laura's face. *"Verde!"* the child whispered. *"Verde . . . muy buenita . . ."*

"What?" Laura asked, puzzled.

"Ah!" Theil said with a nod. "It's your eyes. She's never seen green eyes before." Laura winked and Mara smiled again.

"So, Mara, may I pray for you?" Michael asked. The girl nodded, transferring her gaze to Michael's face. She took a few more shuddering breaths and Michael touched her head and asked God's healing for her.

Afterward, in Theil's cramped office, the man explained, in clipped Nordic phrasing, "Mara is one of the favors I need from you, Michael."

"How can I help?"

"She's very sick. It's her heart. A congenital defect. It's a miracle she's still alive. She needs an operation and I've arranged for one in La Paz. The problem is, I need someone I can trust to transport her there."

"The plane leaves for La Paz weekly . . ." Michael said.

"True. But Helga and I can't take her. There are too many responsibilities here. She'll need constant oxygen, constant monitoring until the ambulance picks her up at the airport. Perhaps Billy and Lisa could handle this. You're due to leave tomorrow."

It was true. The week of crusades were over. They were all due to fly out the next day. Everything had gone very smoothly since that first encounter with Sanchez—except that both Jack and Phil had contracted a virus. Theil had given them medication, but "waiting it out" was his best medical advice. Now little Mara was a further complication.

Theil dropped his eyes and fumbled with some

147

papers on his desk. "That brings me to the rest of my request . . ." he said with hesitancy. "Since you have a pilot's license . . . I was wondering . . . if perhaps you could fly some supplies into Inga's farm at San Ramon . . ."

Michael threw back his head and laughed. His blue eyes danced and twinkled. "I would consider it an honor!" he said.

Theil cast him a sheepish grin. "Helga told me you would. I'm very grateful, Michael. Sometimes I feel there's not enough of me to go around . . ." Laura sensed his frustration.

"It's not a long flight," Theil added with renewed enthusiasm. "About two hours from here over the grasslands. Leave in the morning, have lunch with Inga, and you'll be back in La Paz before dinner. A quick and simple trip by air—two weeks on the ground. No roads," he explained with a shrug.

Laura felt a momentary pang of disappointment. She didn't want to be separated from Michael. Not even for a day. Yet, Phil and Jack were both ill. She and Chris would have to help them. Lisa and Billy would have their hands full watching over Mara. Since Enrique spoke Mara's language, he would also be needed to comfort and calm the child. Laura would just have to face the flight back over the mountains, while Michael flew to San Ramon alone.

"I will contact Inga by radio and let her know when to expect you," Theil said, rising from behind his desk. "I must also get the supplies together. And I need to make arrangements for Mara with Dr. Manzon at the Victor Paz Estensorro Hospital. We've discussed her case many times. I know he can help her."

Theil paused. "We will go out to the airfield later today so that you may check out the plane and prepare everything. Oh, and Michael," the older man added thoughtfully, 'it would be good to take someone with you. It's only a one-day trip, but it would be best not to go alone."

In unison, both men looked at Laura. Her heart skipped a beat and she felt suddenly weak. "Oh no . . . she started, shaking her head emphatically. But the slow smile that flickered across Michael's face told her she'd already lost the battle.

Laura gripped the sides of the seat in the small single-engine plane and stared straight ahead into the bright blue sky. It wasn't that she was scared. She was terrified! The tiny aircraft was nothing like the sleek Lear jet of Garland Enterprises. Its engines purred discreetly. Its seats were plush and cushioned. It had a stocked galley, a crew of three, and a lavatory.

Theil Swensen's Helio Courier was compact and old—its instrument panel a maze of old-fashioned gauges and needles. Laura could hardly think above the roar of the engine. The red-winged plane seemed to hit every air pocket and perverse air current, causing her to feel jostled and disoriented. Below, the flat grasslands of the Bolivian savannas flashed along, broken by an occasional cluster of trees and scrubby palmettoes.

She took a sidelong glance at Michael. He seemed to be enjoying himself, his hands on the controls, the radio headphones clamped tightly to his ears. "Isn't this great!" he yelled above the din.

Laura tried hard to sound enthusiastic. "Yes!" she called. "Great!" But secretly, she wished they were both sitting on the metal bench seats lining the inside of the old DC-3 that had ferried the rest of their group back to La Paz.

Yet she also knew that the trip had been necessary. Inga Swensen had badly needed the medical supplies they'd packed in the cargo hold of the small plane. Laura could still see the big rawboned woman in her

149

mind's eye. How pleased she'd been to see them. How excited over the boxes of goods and supplies. She'd been like a child at Christmas, clapping her hands in delight over every newly opened box.

She'd invited them to share a simple lunch of thick soup containing yucca, onions, green bananas, and potatoes, cooked on the open fire of the home she shared with a family of six. If the conditions in Magdalena had seemed primitive to Laura, the reality of San Ramon was like something out of ancient history books.

There, Laura saw poverty that all but overwhelmed her. Six, eight, ten people living in one-room huts. People in threadbare clothes patched together in a crazy quiltwork of old material. Children, barefoot, dirty, playing in ditches with only rocks for toys.

"I'm the only medical authority for hundreds of kilometers," Inga had explained. "And I'm just a nurse. Sometimes people walk for days to have me check them. Usually, by the time it's serious enough for *La Medica*—that's me—it's too late. I often pray that God would bless them with a doctor, a clinic, a school. Some of these little ones join their parents in the farm fields when they are only ten years old. Ah, Michael . . ." Inga had shaken her head and thrown up her roughened hands in resignation, "there's so much to do! So few hours in the day!"

Michael listened intently, his blue eyes pensive while Inga spoke. Laura knew that he, too, had often been inundated by the magnitude of the work that needed to be done in these mission fields.

They had stayed as long as they dared in San Ramon. It was necessary to get back in the air and on course for La Paz by midafternoon. Yet, when they left, Michael gave his promise that he would be back in touch with Inga in the weeks to come. Now, with their flight course set, they headed toward the mountains and a life far away from the hot, dry savannas and grasslands.

Laura attempted to relax. It would be four hours before they reached La Paz. But she was uncomfortable. It was more than the tiny plane. It was a nagging sense of foreboding. A feeling that somehow, something wasn't quite right . . . She heard it first. A hesitancy in the plane's engine. She leaned forward and cocked her ear.

There! She heard it again. The engine was definitely sputtering. She turned questioning eyes toward Michael. Michael pulled back the earphones and tapped on several gauges. The engine sputtered one more time, then quit altogether.

The sudden impact of total silence left Laura numb. "Michael . . ." she gasped.

"Shh!" he commanded. He tried to restart the engine. It wouldn't catch. Laura watched, fascinated in a macabre way, as the whirling propeller slowed and then stopped spinning.

Michael pulled back on the wheel, forcing the nose of the plane up. Its dead-weight descent slowed. He quickly lowered the flaps, slowing the plane even more.

"Michael, please . . ." Laura begged.

His jaw muscles tightened, but his voice sounded controlled. "Listen to me, Laura," he demanded. "I've got to set her down."

"But there's no place to land!" Laura cried, her eyes swiftly scanning the sea of grass below.

"Then I'll make a place!" he shouted. "I'll keep her gliding as long as I can. The slower we go down, the easier the landing. But this baby's got fixed landing gear," he continued, concentrating on keeping the nose up and settling the plane as gently as he could. "That means that when she hits, the tires will probably buckle. If the struts break, she'll tip."

Laura stifled a cry.

"Stop it!" he commanded. "Just do *exactly* as I tell you."

She nodded mutely, watching the ever-looming ground flash by beneath them . . . faster and faster . . . closer and closer. "Get those pillows and blankets from behind your seat. Stuff them all around your face and body. Put one pillow across your face." His commands came in rapid-fire succession. She hurriedly struggled to obey them, willing herself to concentrate.

"Now when we hit, keep the pillow over your face until the plane has come to a dead stop."

"But, Michael . . ." she cried.

"Do you understand?"

"Yes," she said, her voice cracking.

"Once we've completely stopped, get out and away from the plane." His voice drilled the instructions like bullets.

She nodded again and pulled the pillow up across her face, blocking out the daylight. Now there was only darkness. Her body was surrounded by padding, and she felt like a moth in a too-tight cocoon. Her only link with the nightmare was sound. Somewhere in the distance she could hear Michael speaking into the radio.

"Mayday! Mayday! This is Victor 9H8000 . . ." He gave out some more numbers, then described their surroundings, their point of origin, their destination. She heard the sound of wind rushing past. Felt the descent of the plane, like a wounded bird helplessly caught in a downdraft. Or a runaway elevator hurtling toward the bottom of the shaft. She hugged the pillow tighter to her face.

Suddenly, without warning, the plane hit the ground. It bounced, tossing her forward into the cushion of the blankets, causing her body to strain violently against her seatbelt. There was a crunching sound, a series of thuds and thumps. She heard the

152

sound of glass crunching . . . felt a sickening surge in the pit of her stomach . . . heard a violent rending, as of metal being torn . . . felt the plane nose forward, lurch, tip sideways. She screamed, muffling her anguish into the pillow.

Then there was no motion. No sounds. Only silence.

## CHAPTER 10

EVER SO SLOWLY Laura lowered the pillow. She was looking at a world gone cockeyed, topsy-turvy, at sharp angles. She blinked and shook her head. Then she realized that she was almost lying on her side. That the plane had tipped forward and over. She unsnapped her seat restraint and struggled to sit upright.

She looked over at the pilot's seat. Her heart skipped wildly. "Michael!" she cried. But he didn't respond. His head seemed pressed into the window beside him. A web of cracked but intact glass glittered ominously where he leaned against it.

"Oh, Michael!" She struggled to crawl out of the seat next to him. Managing to grasp the back of his seat, she pulled herself alongside his motionless body. Her heart thudded and her hands trembled. "Dear God . . ." she prayed aloud. "Please don't let him be . . ." She couldn't say the word.

Gently she reached out her hand and touched his cheek. He moaned. Relief coursed through her. He was alive! She remembered his warning then. "Get out of the plane. Get away from it . . ."

"Come on, Michael . . ." she urged, pulling at him. His head fell back against the seat. It was then that she saw the blood. Her hands and heart froze. Why was there so much blood? She strained to reach over him to see the side of his head.

"You're hurt, Michael," she explained, more for her own benefit than for his, "but you've got to get out." He didn't move. Laura unbuckled his seat belt and pulled him forward. "Please . . . Michael . . ." she whispered. "Please . . . help me. I can't do it alone . . ."

"Laura?" At the sound of her name, waves of gratitude washed over her. "Are you all right?" He kept trying to focus his eyes, but the effort seemed too great for him.

"I'm fine," she said quickly. "But you're cut and bleeding. Michael . . . please . . . I need your help if I'm going to get you out of the plane."

He lay back, and for a minute she thought he'd slipped into unconsciousness. But slowly, he leaned forward and she managed to help him out of his seat. Together they squeezed toward the door. The plane was tipped in such a way that the door wasn't jammed, but once Laura opened it, the drop to the ground seemed impossible.

She closed her eyes and jumped. Then she turned and reached up for Michael. Somehow he made it out, but the exertion left him weak. She saw the gash on his head clearly now. It looked deep and angry, a large blue-black lump rising beneath it.

"Come on, Michael," she pleaded. She half-lifted, half-dragged him toward an enormous tree about 150 yards from the fallen plane. With one final thrust of strength, she propped him against the tree, then collapsed in a heap beside him, shaking with exhaustion.

Finally she crouched forward next to him and tried

155

to rouse him. "Michael?" she said gently. "We made it! We got away from the plane."

He opened his eyes briefly. "I knew you could . . ." His eyes closed again. "I just need to rest a few minutes . . ." his voice trailed off and she watched helplessly. Michael couldn't help her now. What was she going to do? Dear God . . . what was she going to do?

She looked around. As far as she could see, the land stretched flat and grassy. It was a long, brownish grass, not thick and soft as she'd imagined from the air, but sparse and sharp. Its lushness was only an illusion. It was really dry, brown, unfriendly grass.

The tree above them was an old mango tree, reaching high into the late afternoon sky. Nearby Laura saw a cluster of palmettoes and a few scrubby trees. The plane—tipped and broken, its wing sheared off, its nose in the grass, its propeller bent—resembled a wounded albatross.

"What am I going to do?" she asked aloud. Only the hum of insects replied. She looked back at Michael. He still had not moved. She was all he had. Only Laura Garland stood between him and certain death. She began to cry.

Suddenly she wiped her hand across her eyes. "Stop it!" she commanded herself. "Think! Stop feeling sorry and scared and *think!*"

The first thing she needed to do was go back to the plane and bring out everything of value—everything she could possibly use to help Michael. Surely there was a first aid kit on board. Theil was a doctor. Of course, he'd have a kit on the plane! The thought spurred her to action.

"Michael," she said to his still figure, "I'll be right back." When he didn't respond, she touched him lightly and scurried back to the plane.

It took several trips, but eventually she brought all the pillows and blankets she'd used to cushion her landing, a first aid kit, and a third container that held

156

an axe, a knife, matches, a gallon of water, several tins of C-rations, some dried beef jerky, a compass, and a Bible. A small smile played over her lips as she ran her hand over the smooth black surface of the leather-bound book.

On her final trip, she found a sleeping bag. Good! Quickly she spread it flat on the ground. Then she dragged Michael on top of it. At least he would be more comfortable. She opened the first aid kit and rummaged through its contents. There were vials of medicine, syringes, creams, bandages, and alcohol.

Well, she couldn't give him a shot or suture the cut, but she could clean it and wrap it and protect it from the buzzing insects. Laura worked quickly, and in a little while, Michael's head was swathed in clean white gauze, the ugly lump protected and hidden. He'd opened his eyes several times while she worked, but each time lapsed again into unconsciousness. Once she'd done all she knew to do, she let him rest.

Surely someone had heard Michael's Mayday, she told herself over and over. Surely they realized back in La Paz that the plane was overdue. Since they had the flight plan, a rescue party would be sent out to look for them. But how far off course had they ventured, looking for a place to set the plane down? She wouldn't think of that now. It was too frightening.

No . . . she'd concentrate on making their surroundings as comfortable as possible . . . on cheerful thoughts and positive prayers . . . on listening for the familiar drone of a rescue plane.

Laura sat, gripping her knees to her chest, and stared at Michael. She didn't know much about head injuries, but she was sure he had a concussion. The lump and bruise on his head attested to that fact. Why didn't he wake up? Why didn't he talk to her? She crawled next to him and very gently touched his cheek. Already, it was rough with a stubble of whiskers.

"Michael . . ." she said softly. He tried to respond,

but the struggle sapped his energy. After a few more minutes, she called his name again. This time he managed to open his eyes. The effort seemed very great.

"Laura . . ." he whispered.

She offered him a drink. He sipped the water and then closed his eyes, exhausted. In another few minutes, he opened them again and directed, "In the plane . . . under the seat. Get my gun . . ."

She nodded and returned to the plane. It took a few minutes, but finally her fingers closed around a leather holster. In it was a pistol. It looked cold and dark and ominous, but she carried it to Michael, cradling it in her hands, afraid it might discharge.

"Here . . ." she told Michael.

He forced his eyes open again. "I'm not sure if I can stay awake . . ." he confessed. "If there's trouble . . . you have to shoot."

*Trouble?* she thought. *What kind of trouble? Michael, please . . .* her mind screamed. *Help me!* Aloud she asked, "What do you want me to do?"

He talked her through the firing of the pistol. Told her how to release the safety; how to cock it. "If you fire, keep your elbows locked. There'll be quite a kick. And a loud noise . . ."

*Dear God,* she pleaded, *don't let me have to fire.*

"Time?" he asked weakly.

"Five o'clock," she told him. At least her watch still worked.

"Night . . ." he said with a pained grimace. "Build a fire . . ."

It hit her then. There would be no rescue this day. The best they could hope for was that someone would come for them tomorrow. They would have to spend the night here—here in the hostile world of the Bolivian grasslands—with only a few C-rations, some blankets, and her wits.

*Build a fire. How does one build a fire?* she asked herself. There were matches in the one kit. But she'd have to find the material to burn. Laura fought down the rising panic. *I can't build a fire . . . I can't.*

"You've got to!" she told herself fiercely. "There's no one else . . ."

At least the weather was warm. They wouldn't freeze to death. So she had to assume that the fire was for their protection—like the gun . . .

She set to work gathering small tree branches. The larger limbs, she hacked at with the axe. Slowly, she piled up a supply of firewood. She pulled and tugged at the dried palmettoes, wrestling with them until her hands were cut and bleeding. She went back to the plane and pulled apart wooden cargo boxes until she had a heap of stuff that would burn.

But how much wood was enough? How long would it last? Through the night? Grimly, Laura ran her hands over the butt of the gun.

"All right," she said aloud. "I have a pile of wood. Now what?"

There was no answer. Michael had drifted off again into some twilight world, away from his pain and their dilemma. "I wish I'd joined the Girl Scouts," she muttered darkly, trying to decide how to logically attack the fire-building problem.

Laura forced every picture she'd ever seen of a campfire into her brain. Perhaps if she could remember what one looked like, she could duplicate it. She dug around in the supply kit and found a small shovel. "They must have put this in for just such emergencies . . ." she told herself. But what to do with it?

A trench! Yes . . . that made sense. She'd have to dig around the place where she wanted to build the fire. The grass was so dry. She didn't want to risk starting a grassland fire. A trough would contain the flames to the specific area.

She selected a spot near the foot of the blanket where Michael lay, cleared out all the grass she could pull up by hand, and began to dig.

After an hour, she had created a circle of dirt and

smooth ground. In the center of the cleared circle, she heaped thicker branches, palmetto fronds, and small twigs.

She backed off and observed her handiwork. "It looks good," she assured herself. "Ah . . . but will it burn?" Hastily, she tore off some strips of cloth and piled them on the heap, too. Then she very carefully struck a match and set the cloth afire.

The material caught at once, but after it was consumed by the flames, the fire quickly died out. *Try again,* she told herself through clenched teeth. But this time, she heaped dry grass onto the pile and stuck handfuls of it toward the bottom of the pile. The grass caught instantly, burning brightly, and flamed long enough to catch the smaller twigs and finally the larger, bottom branches. A thin spiral of smoke rose, leaving its thick smoky essence in her nostrils.

"I did it, Michael!" Laura beamed, watching the fire burn and crackle. He didn't stir. She suddenly thought of Mac. *What would you think of me, Mac, if you could see me now?* A wave of loneliness washed over her again. She shook her head. *No time to dwell on that . . .*

Next, she ate some of the beef jerky. It tasted dry and salty, but it did take the edge off her gnawing hunger. She leaned back against the tree, sitting near Michael's head and gazing longingly at his face. The sky streaked with the waning rays of the setting sun. In a few minutes, it would be dark.

Laura watched as the sky deepened from reds to purples and then watched as a vast canopy of velvet blackness descended over her head. Thousands of twinkling stars flickered on and sprinkled their jeweled brightness across the face of the darkness. She felt awed and insignificant . . . and alone.

*If I start to cry now,* she told herself, *I won't stop.* She put a few more branches on the fire, focusing on the dancing, shimmering flames. She couldn't let the fire go out. It had to keep burning. Michael was counting on her and she couldn't let him down. Somehow, the task took on religious proportions.

She absently picked up the Bible and flipped through its pages. A few minutes' reading left her feeling oddly strengthened. They weren't alone out there, after all. God was with them. The thought reassured her and she closed her eyes in silent prayer.

Then she heard the noise. The hair on her arms bristled. Perhaps she was mistaken. No . . . she heard it again. Something rustling through the bushes. She had assumed that they were all alone. Now, the unpleasant thought crossed her mind that something else was out there . . . watching them. Something that wasn't afraid of the night. Something that was accustomed to the darkness.

Cautiously Laura reached over and ran her hand along the side of the blanket, never taking her eyes off the clump of bushes from which the sound had emanated. Her hand touched the cool leather holster. Slowly she drew the heavy pistol out of its protective sheath and rose to her knees.

She snapped off the safety. It made a soft click. A twig snapped from within the clump of bushes. "Go away . . ." she half whispered. No answer. "I mean it!" she said, trying hard to control her quavering voice. "I-I have a gun . . ."

She raised the pistol, cocked it, and held it in both her trembling hands. She locked her elbows. And then she saw the eyes reflected in the firelight—yellow, narrow, gleaming. They were set wide apart and though she never saw a body, she had the impression of "cat." Her heart thumped wildly.

Laura rose shakily, spread her feet, and aimed the gun toward the bushes, at the spot where she'd seen the eyes. "Go away!" she shouted. Then she fired. The gun boomed in her ears, the repercussion pushing her physically backward. Her hands stung and tingled. All around her, the night grew instantly quiet. No insects stirred. No night creatures called to one another.

Michael called feverishly, "Laura!" She dropped to her knees next to him and touched his face reassuringly.

"It's all right," she said over and over. "I just scared off some animal . . ."

It was true. She no longer heard the rustling in the bushes. Slowly the sounds of the night resumed their melodies, like a reluctant chorus—the insects, the frogs, the night birds. Laura exhaled deeply, resnapped the safety on the gun, and slid it into its holster.

She sat for a long time, staring into the fire. Every so often, she threw a branch onto the low flames. Finally her eyelids grew heavy with sleep. She fought to remain conscious. What if the animal came back? "I must stay awake . . ." she commanded herself. But her eyelids kept drooping, begging for rest.

Once again, her eyes sought Michael's face. How still he lay. Long brown fingers of shadow reached across his features. His eyes were like sunken hollows and his beard pushed through, creating a dark cast over his face and chin. The bandage cut a white swath through his dark hair, stray locks trailing over its edges.

Her heart ached for him. Softly, she leaned over him. Very gently, she leaned down and kissed his mouth, her lips pressing longingly against his. He never stirred. She touched the side of his face, trailing her fingers down his firm, square-cut jaw, as if memorizing every detail. So close . . . so close . . . yet, so still . . .

Tenderly, ever so slowly, Laura curled up next to his long, lean, sleeping body. She could feel his warmth—the muscular hardness of his limbs.

She bent her head over his mouth and nose, listening to his shallow breathing, feeling his breath warm against her cheek. When she lay her head on his

162

chest, she heard the rhythmic thumping of his heart. His nearness comforted her. A deep and dreamless sleep overtook her . . .

The uncomfortable dampness of predawn soaked into Laura's consciousness and began to rouse her. She woke languidly, still curled up next to Michael, her body pressed tightly against his. As she became more and more aware of her surrounding, she struggled to the surface of wakefulness, until she was fully alert. She hesitated to move, fearful of disturbing Michael and feeling guilty for being so close to his warm and comforting body.

She eased up and scooted away, glancing down at his sleeping form. Stiff and sore all over, she rubbed her eyes and glanced toward the fire. All that remained of it was a few smoldering embers. Reprimanding herself for allowing it to die down, she poked at it, threw more fuel onto it, and was rewarded when it smoked and caught, the tiny red-yellow flames eagerly licking the new fuel, chasing away the damp chill that had settled on her.

Her survey of the surroundings in the gray light proved the bushes to be friendlier, not ominous and threatening as they had the night before. With a shudder, she recalled the sound of something's moving in the bushes, her fright, the glimpse of yellow eyes, the feel and the sound of the pistol in her hands.

Laura stood and stretched. Evidently the plane's forced landing had affected her, after all. She felt sore, bruised; her head pounded, and the pit of her stomach gurgled hollow and empty.

In the light of early morning the plane resembled a giant behemoth, broken and bent, a torn and twisted hulk, void of purpose and function. Poor Theil! His plane was lost to him forever! Laura walked around the area cautiously, exercising her protesting muscles.

The ground was damp with dew. She watched a spider climb over his web, the little clinging droplets of moisture giving the structure the appearance of a jeweled crown. The rich, damp smell of earth filled her nostrils. High above in the trees, she heard the chattering of monkeys, squawking and scrambling from limb to limb. The pink-red of dawn dispersed the grayness of the night, and soon the oblique rays of the sun broke through the overhead tree branches.

Laura's mind began to race. Would a rescue party find them today? Would they ever see them in this vast wilderness? How was she going to manage until help came? Would Michael be all right?

Surely God knew how much they needed Him . . . Surely He would not forsake them . . . She shook her head, trying hard to clear it. No use thinking fearful thoughts. She had to keep her wits—had to be strong. Their survival depended on it.

Back on the blanket, sitting next to Michael, she placed her hand on his forehead. The pressure caused his eyes to open. She felt a flood of gratitude and smiled softly at him. "Hello, stranger . . . How do you feel?"

He stared blankly at her for a moment and then, with tremendous effort, focused his attention on speaking. "My . . . my head hurts . . ." he mumbled.

"I don't doubt it. You took a nasty bang." She paused. "How about a little water?"

He nodded and she poured some of the precious liquid into a cup and held it while he took small sips. The effort left him pale and weak. "Do you think you could eat something?" she asked eagerly.

"I don't know . . ." he said hesitantly.

"I have some beef jerky." She offered it to him. "It tastes like shoe leather, but it's filling." He took some of it and chewed it cautiously. "I kept a fire going all night . . ." she told him, mostly to keep him awake and functioning.

He gave her a half-smile. "A regular Girl Scout . . ."

She laughed. "I'm afraid I'll never earn a merit

164

badge. In my neighborhood, we have servants to take the tests . . ."

He reached out and grasped her hand. "I don't know if anyone heard my 'Mayday'," he said on a serious note.

"I keep hoping someone will come for us . . ." she said, dropping her eyes so that he wouldn't see the fear in them.

"The radio?" he asked.

Hope leaped up within her. "Why . . . I never thought to see if it was working," she confessed. "Besides, I don't know how to use it."

"Check it. See that it's tuned to 121.5 . . . that's the emergency frequency . . ." he told her with considerable effort. "Push in the button . . . hold it close to your mouth . . . ask for help."

Laura nodded, her pulse racing with anticipation. She hurried back to the plane, crawled inside and picked up the radio microphone, checking it carefully. Everything looked intact. She twisted the dial until the indicator needle pointed to 121.5, pushed in the button, and said, "Help us. This is Laura Garland. Michael Raintree and I are down on the ground somewhere between San Ramon and La Paz. Michael's hurt. Does anyone hear me?"

She released the button. There was no response. She repeated the message three more times. Each time, she waited for the radio to crackle with an answer. Each time she was disappointed. "It's no use," she told Michael, returning to him beneath the tree.

"Maybe you can't receive," he said. "That doesn't mean someone didn't hear you . . ."

"You think so?" she asked anxiously. "Oh, Michael . . ." she confessed, tears brimming in her eyes. "I'm scared. I wish I were like you, had more faith . . . But—but I don't."

"Hey!" he said, gripping her hand with concentrated effort. "It's Okay. Don't lose hope. Laura," he told her, "God didn't bring us all the way to Bolivia to let us die in the grasslands." His voice faltered with the exertion of speaking and she nodded gratefully, ashamed of her outburst.

"Why don't I check your head wound?" she asked. Gingerly she unwound the bandage, exposing the gash and bump. The wound looked purple and ugly and there was a telltale reddening at the base of the cut. Infection might be setting in.

Quickly she washed it again in alcohol. Michael grimaced. "Sorry," she told him, as she rewrapped it in fresh, clean gauze and cotton.

"Didn't know you were a nurse, too."

"Shh . . ." she cautioned. "Don't tire yourself. Maybe you'd better rest . . ."

But his eyes had already closed and he had drifted back into his semiconscious state. Loneliness filled her. She missed the fellowship of his company. Would this nightmare never end?

The sun climbed high overhead and by noon, her hunger had become ferocious. Laura opened one of the tins of the C-rations and sniffed its contents suspiciously. It looked and smelled unappetizing, but she ate it anyway and was amazed that it tasted better than it appeared.

She took a long drink of water, measuring the precious liquid and what was left of it in its plastic container. They couldn't make it without water. Once this was gone . . . Maybe she'd better look for some . . . Her eye fell on a clump of scrub brush. Funny, she'd never seen that clump before. Never really *looked* at it.

"It's cabbage palm!" she said aloud after she'd observed it more closely. Deep within its prickly interior lay a succulent, tender morsel of edible vegetable. Her memory went back to the time she'd sat in the elegant Coral Gables restaurant and nonchalantly eaten the hearts of palm salad, served on a chilled plate, nestled on a bed of crisp lettuce, drizzled with a tangy vinaigrette dressing. Her mouth watered at the memory. How ironic!

Now, she stood examining the origin of the delicious delicacy in its natural surroundings, protected, guarded by sharp-pointed fronds. How long ago . . . How far away . . . How much she'd taken for granted. But if she had to, she would hack the cabbage palm away until she uncovered the middle. It was a source of food—of life itself.

The afternoon sun beat down, leaving Laura feeling limp and listless. She longed to take a nice cool bath . . . or even to wash her face with scented soap. But as uncomfortable as she felt, she knew that Michael must feel even more so. She rearranged the pillows for greater succor, opened his shirt and sponged his neck and chest with alcohol and, fanned him with a towel to relieve him of the unrelenting heat.

Twice Michael asked for water. She gave him small sips from the cup, then dampened the ends of a cloth and stroked his brow and face. By now, his beard was quite distinct, giving him a look of rugged darkness. He could be a pioneer, a woodsman from another world.

She grew more and more concerned. He seemed feverish now and she feared for him, praying frequently for his safety, his healing. How she longed for a doctor to treat him.

As the long day wore on, her hopes of imminent rescue dimmed. By late afternoon, she knew she'd have to gather more wood for another fire—another fire to guard against the night creatures. She began her search for fuel, working her way out into an ever-widening circle. This second day wood was not so easy to find. She'd already exhausted the supply in the immediate vicinity.

By the time she'd scrounged enough, the rays of the setting sun streaked across the sky. She opened another tin of C-rations and ate it hungrily. The physical labor had left her ravenous, but she determined to eat only what was absolutely necessary. She had no way of knowing how long they would be here. She had to conserve—had to force herself to live on survival rations.

Laura thought of all the food she'd wasted in her lifetime, taking for granted the sheer abundance of her lifestyle. She thought of the meals she'd skipped, the food she'd ignored and thrown out. What she'd give for some of that excess right now!

She built the fire again, watching it blaze and dance in the darkening night. She brought the pistol closer to her side, caressing the cold steel assurance of its barrel. She was not nearly so afraid of it tonight. Out here, it was a friend.

Once again, she struggled to stay awake as long as possible. Every time her head drooped, she'd jerk awake and cautiously look around. She didn't want to be caught off guard. But whatever had come to inspect them the night before did not return. For that she was grateful and she thanked God quietly.

In the very early hours of the morning, Laura again inched closer to Michael, curling herself into the hollow of his side and falling into a fitful sleep. The sun was high, its rays stabbing her eyes, when she awoke with a start the next morning. Michael stared down at her, his violet-blue gaze caressing her face.

She scrambled away from him, her cheeks burning, like a child caught red-handed. "I-I'm sorry . . ." she mumbled, trying to smooth her hair and, at the same time, apologize for snuggling close to him. He attempted a smile. His lips, parched and dry, parted in amusement. His eyes, bright and glowing, penetrated to her core, stripping her feelings bare. Could she never escape those soul-revealing eyes of his?

"No problem," he told her softly. "I think I'll try some more of that beef jerky." He changed the topic adroitly. She gave him some, but after a few mouthfuls, he handed it back. "Harder to chew than I remembered . . ." Pain showed on his face.

168

"Does your head still hurt?"

"Yes," he said tersely, then fell back, exhausted. His thick dark lashes closed over his eyes, and deep furrows lined his forehead.

"I need to change the bandage," she said. "The cut might be getting infected."

"Maybe later . . ."

She heard a faint noise. At first it sounded like an overgrown insect droning in the midmorning heat. "Michael!" she cried. "I-I hear something . . . Maybe it's a plane!" She leaped up and ran from under the protection of the tree, out into the clearing. Scanning the blue sky anxiously, all she saw were clusters of white clouds and the intense burning ball of the sun.

But the sound was growing louder. Laura trotted around in a circle, never taking her eyes off the sky. Then, she saw the aircraft, flying low in deliberate criss-cross patterns. She began to shout and wave her arms. *Please let them see me,* she prayed silently.

She hurried back to the tree and scrambled for a large towel. "Michael!" she cried. "It's a plane! I saw it! I saw it!" She raced back into the clearing and waved the towel frantically.

"O dear God . . ." she prayed. "Let them see our plane. Let them find us!" She could see the single-engine craft quite plainly now. It circled lazily overhead, moving in huge circles.

She continued to wave the towel. Then, as if in silent acknowledgment, the plane's wing dipped, like a large dragonfly investigating its prey. They had seen her! She continued to watch as the pilot circled back overhead, descending lower and lower, looking for a place to set down.

At last the plane landed, bumping to a stop along the grassy field. Laura watched, her heart in her throat, afraid that this plane, too, might break apart on the rugged terrain. But it didn't. She began running toward it even before the engine completely shut off.

The door opened and Billy Powell jumped out and

raced to her. When he reached her, she fell into his arms, sobbing with gratitude and relief. "It's all right . . ." he said over and over, in his soft Southern accent. His quiet brown eyes raced over her, full of questions. But all he said was, "It's all right . . ."

There were two other men, kind and helpful, with water and food and bandages. They examined Michael, lifted him onto a stretcher, and secured it on the plane. Laura boarded with Billy, all the while talking, crying, rambling of their three-day ordeal, while his calm, reassuring hands buckled her into her seat.

The plane taxied and lifted quickly, as she watched the ground fall away and the scene of the crash shrink into toylike dimensions as the craft climbed skyward. Exhausted, Laura drifted in and out of wakefulness, soothed by Billy's presence and the lulling drone of the engine. *It's over . . .* she told herself repeatedly. *Thank You, Lord, for saving us.*

The Cessna rose up and up, ever higher over the grasslands, the foothills and finally the majestic mountain peaks surrounding La Paz . . . the city of Peace.

## CHAPTER 11

LAURA WALKED SWIFTLY down the long dimly lit corridor of the hospital. Outside, the city's lights glowed against the night. But here in the La Paz high-rise hospital, there was no sense of time. The corridors were clean and quiet, heavy with the biting smell of antiseptic.

Laura had fallen onto the bed in her hotel room late that afternoon, too exhausted even to undress. She'd begged to go to the hospital with Michael, but a firm and insistent Lisa had practically locked her in her room, commanding her to ". . . get some rest and go later." She'd been too numb to argue.

At eight, Laura had awakened, anxious to know about Michael. So she'd bathed—a wanton luxury that had never felt better—changed, and taken a cab to the giant hospital complex after talking briefly to Billy and Lisa in their room.

"He's resting comfortably," Billy had assured her. "They sutured his head cut, started him on antibiotics, took X-rays, and checked him into a room for observation.

"As you know, Michael has a concussion," Billy had said matter-of-factly. "They'll do an EEG tomorrow to check out his brain waves, but his doctor says that concussions are funny things. Sometimes the victim sleeps it off. Sometimes he loses his memory and behaves erratically. Sometimes there is pain, double vision, even convulsions."

Her face must have betrayed her concern, because Billy had paused and placed his hand on her shoulder and looked her in the eye. "The one thing he needs most of all is absolute rest and quiet," he'd added gently. "They expect Michael to be in the hospital about three days and they'll be checking him over thoroughly. If he recovers quickly, he'll be back in his normal routine as soon as possible." Billy squeezed her shoulder reassuringly. "Now, why don't you go back to your room and sleep? Then, I'll personally take you down there first thing in the morning."

She'd nodded, but decided to ignore Billy's counsel and took a cab to the hospital instead. After getting Michael's room number from the information desk, Laura headed for the elevators. She avoided the nurse's station on his floor and slipped noiselessly inside his room.

The room was dark, illuminated by a single night light. Michael slept, his large frame covered by starched, clean sheets and a lightweight blanket. A thick white bandage covered his left temple and forehead. She stared down at him wistfully.

She longed to touch him. But she didn't want to wake him. She heard the door glide open behind her. Laura turned and came face-to-face with Chris. The two women surveyed each other with guarded wariness.

"I-I wanted to see him . . ." Chris explained haltingly.

Laura nodded, feeling the old jealousies stir. It was obvious that Chris expected her to leave the room.

172

Laura wavered for a moment. But the look on Chris's face, so full of fear and relief and yearning, caused her to back down from any confrontation.

"I was just going . . ." she lied, crossing to the door. Chris quickly took her place at Michael's bedside.

"Laura . . ." Chris called. Laura paused, turning toward the bed. "I-I'm glad you were there to help him . . ." she finished in a whisper.

Laura watched as Chris leaned over Michael's bed and kissed him tenderly. The thick cascade of her hair fell like a veil across his chest and face, obliterating both their features from Laura's gaze. It was as if Laura did not exist. As if she weren't even in the room.

She heard Michael's husky voice: "Hi, pretty lady . . ."

And Chris's reply: "Welcome back. I thought I'd lost you . . ."

Laura felt like an outsider again. An intruder. A voyeur. There was no room for her in their world. The heady scent of Chris's perfume swept away the smells of the hospital. The single light glimmered off her beautiful hair.

As quietly as possible, Laura slipped out of the room, closing the door softly behind her.


"It was sabotage," Billy announced emphatically from the corner of Michael's hospital room while he lifted the blinds, allowing the bright morning sun light to stream into the room.

"What?" Laura asked with disbelief from her chair next to Michael's bed. Perhaps she hadn't heard correctly.

"I'm not surprised," Michael noted from his hospital bed, the back of it raised so that he was in a sitting position. "That plane's engine shut down too neatly for it to have been anything else."

173

" 'Water found in the the fuel tank and in the fuel lines . . .'," Billy read from a paper in his hand. He snorted in disgust and tossed the papers on the table next to Michael's bed.

"I drained those lines myself," Michael said, his blue eyes flashing. He shrugged. "Can't prove it though. My word against the 'Official Report'." He picked up the paper and scanned it quickly.

Laura watched Michael as he spoke. He was clean-shaven now, and a small, neat bandage covered the tiny black suture lines of his cut. The gauntness was gone from his face. He was alert, restless, miraculously recovered from his injury and three-day ordeal. He had thanked her, of course, holding both her hands and gazing deeply into her eyes, for her role in their safety and rescue. But she could not shake the memory of Chris's bending possessively over him two nights before. Chris loved him—even a child could see that. But did Michael love Chris? And what did he feel for Laura? Only gratitude? Her mind churned with questions. Her heart burned with uncertainty.

Laura glanced between the two men and finally found her voice. "Do you know what you're saying?" she asked, her voice barely audible. "You're telling me that someone tried to *kill* you, Michael."

He stared directly at her. "Why does that surprise you?" he asked.

She gripped the arms of her chair until her knuckles whitened; her back, ramrod straight. "Michael . . . that's murder. Who would do such a thing?"

"Laura," he said, more gently. "We are at war with the enemy. Our battle isn't against flesh and blood, but against powers and principalities—against the unseen forces of Satan who are always warring with God for the souls of men. When I preached Christ and salvation to the Bolivians, I attacked Satan's army. Naturally, he's going to fight back."

"But Michael, a flesh-and-blood person sabotaged

174

our plane . . ." she said, trying to make sense of what he was telling her.

"True," he said. "And I suspect that our political adversaries in Magdalena had something to do with it. But I can't prove it. So what *can* I do about it except leave it to heaven?"

She grappled with the problem, struggling to escape its horror and to understand Michael's unconcern.

"If it's any consolation," he told her, leaning over and picking up his Bible, "I read the last chapter. And our side wins."

Billy laughed aloud. "Good point." He beamed. "And frankly, something good did come out of it."

"What possible good could have come from our almost dying?" Laura asked, a little peeved at both men's attitude toward the whole matter.

"For starters," Billy said in a slow drawl, "we're getting calls, letters, money from all over Bolivia and South America. People are mad. They're asking to help. To do something. They're standing with Michael, wanting revival. You see, it's all working out in God's favor."

"Something else has come out of it, too," Michael told them both. They looked at him. Laura could see the bright fire of dedication and commitment spring into his eyes. "I now know what God wants me to do for this country. He wants me to build a hospital and a school in San Ramon. For all the people in the southern part of Bolivia."

She didn't doubt for a minute that he would do it.


As soon as Michael was released from the hospital, he was quickly caught up in a maelstrom of activity. There were appearances, seminars, fund-raising meetings. With every group, he shared his dream, his vision of a San Ramon, based healing complex and school . The dream took shape, gained momentum, took on character and life. Money, letters, pledges of support poured into his headquarters in Rey's Mission church.

Laura kept equally busy writing and rewriting press releases, arranging interviews, answering inquiries and requests, and controlling the flow of information. The Sonshine Singers lent their time and talents to the project, too, appearing and singing for groups and meetings.

All of them fell under the pressure of a deadline— the deadline that marked the end of the Bolivian winter and ushered in the spring, and, with spring, the long, tropical rainy season that would impede the progress of the actual building of the facility in San Ramon.

"Even if we can't start the construction until next year, at least we'll have the money in the bank to go ahead with it," Michael told them all at one of his morning staff meetings. It was at the same meeting that disaster struck.

Billy Powell brought out a letter from the government and shared its contents with them. It was filled with apologetic, carefully worded phrases—very obsequious and very official. Laura had enough experience in the ways of bureaucrats to realize at once what the letter said between its lines and carefully constructed wording.

"In short," Billy sighed tossing the letter on the table in the meeting room, "the government won't O.K. the land purchase in San Ramon."

For a few moments, everyone was too stunned to speak. Then they all spoke at once.

"Hold it!" Michael commanded, raising his hands for silence. "It's a setback. But it's not the end of the project. We'll fight." His long, lean body tensed as he spoke, like a cat ready to spring.

*He loves a good fight,* Laura mused. But she had spent many years in the real estate business. She knew from experience that nothing was more frustrating, and often pointless, than dealing with a government bureaucracy. She turned the problem over and over in her mind, examining it from every angle. Someone—or some political faction—had a lot of influence to sidetrack a project with the obvious grass-roots popularity of Michael's.

First the plane, now the project . . . she knew both were connected. Michael was right. The enemy was out to stop him and his work in Bolivia. Out to halt the spread of the gospel, the conversion of the people to the kingdom of God.

She waited until the two of them were alone in the room. She approached him nervously. She had an idea, but it would take his approval and backing. "Laura," he said, smiling. He reached out and touched her cheek. The old familiar tingle shot up her spine.

She stepped backward, forcing her concentration on what she had to say. She mustn't get sidetracked, either. "I-I think I can help cut the red tape . . ." she ventured uneasily.

He surveyed her with interest, his blue eyes narrowing. "I'm listening."

She tipped her chin, took a deep breath and began slowly, deliberately, "My father . . . h-he has contacts, friends in Washington, holdings in South America. If I asked him, he might be able to help . . ." She never finished.

"Forget it!" Michael snapped, crossing his arms over his chest.

Laura's back stiffened and her eyebrow arched. She dug in with renewed determination. "Michael, don't turn me down before you hear me out. I don't know if he can help. I don't know if he even will help . . ." she shrugged. "But at least let me ask . . ."

"I mean it," Michael warned coolly. "I don't want

anything from your father, Laura. Do you understand? Nothing. No favors."

At once, she saw him as unreasonable and unyielding. After all they had been through together! How dare he receive her suggestion like that. How dare he dismiss it as if it had no merit or value!

Her own anger bubbled to the surface and erupted hotly. "Do you know what your problem is, Michael Raintree? You're arrogant, proud, and stubborn! You told us all that this project was a mandate from the Lord! Who are you to refuse *any* avenue to accomplish it?"

He glowered at her. "Don't push me, Laura," he warned. "I don't want anything from Mac Garland. Is that clear?"

"*I'm* from Mac Garland!" she snapped.

Instantly a stony, frozen silence fell between them. The muscles in Michael's jawline tensed. His eyes turned guarded and cold. Yet, he said nothing. Laura glared at him. Her words lay like a gauntlet between them. She didn't wait for him to pick it up. She turned sharply on her heel and stalked angrily out of the room.

She didn't know how she got there, but at one point in the afternoon she found herself in the Plaza Venezuela, the place where Michael had first brought her one afternoon, months before. The specter of her father had driven them there that day, too. It seemed only fitting that she should return.

The air smelled clean and cool. Sun and shadow patterns flickered across the sheet of green grass. Pigeons fluttered from trees and benches. Memories, long dormant, came flooding into her mind. She remembered an afternoon in Biscayne Park—a cool, long-ago day when she'd first encountered the man, Michael. A man with violet-blue eyes, black hair, and the presence of authority. A man whose voice, whose

178

words, stopped traffic and changed lives. Her life, for one.

And she saw Chris in her mind's eye. Beautiful, talented, committed to Michael. She saw them laughing together at Billy and Lisa's wedding. She saw them talking. She saw them touching . . .

"Laura . . ."

Someone had called her name. She turned, unsure of who had summoned her. She came face-to-face with Michael. He was real. No imaginary being. No figment of her memory. "How . . . how did you know where I was . . . ?" she stammered. "I didn't even know . . ." Her shock at seeing him left her groping for words.

Michael stood in front of her, a breeze playing with his hair, his hands thrust in his pockets. "I just knew . . ." he said softly.

Tears brimmed in her eyes. Seeing him, her anger dissipated, causing her to feel ashamed. "I-I'm sorry," she began. "I had no right to talk to you like that . . ."

"You have every right," he said, silencing her. "I *was* arrogant. All that matters is the project. Not my pride. If your father can help . . ."

She looked quickly into his eyes. For a moment it seemed as if they were the only two people in the Plaza, the only two people in the world.

"Ask him . . ." Michael urged. His eyes burned holes in her.

"I-I don't *know* if he can help," she stammered. "But it's worth a try. If he'll see me . . ."

"There's more to it than just asking for aid for my project, isn't there?"

She floundered helplessly for a moment, confused, unsure of his meaning. "What?"

"You have to go back, don't you? For your own sake."

She stood, stunned, astounded by the perception of

179

his comment—the revelation of her innermost thoughts. His words had exposed and reopened the old wound. The minute he said it, she knew it was true. She *had* to go back. She had to see Mac again—to make her peace with him.

"Michael . . ." her voice quavered. "He's my father . . . I still love him."

Michael kept silent, studying her like a scientist scrutinizing a profound dilemma. He nodded slowly. "Yes," he said. "I see that now."

Confused, she wondered, *What does he mean?* Surely, Michael, of all people, understood. She must go to Mac! If only to ask his forgiveness—to rebuild their broken relationship. Michael must know that she'd return to Bolivia as soon as possible. "I-I'll make arrangements to leave tomorrow," she told him.

"Fine," he said.

They fell into step together, and walked toward the stand of taxis, from which one would take them back to the hotel. Why did she feel so uneasy? It was as if a great gulf had opened up between them. She couldn't understand why she felt so removed from Michael. So cut off. His face had settled into an inscrutable mask. She could not read this thoughts. She did not know his heart.


Laura felt like a being from another time, another era, snatched rudely from a quieter, more peaceful existence and tossed into some other world—a foreign, surrealistic world that left her disoriented. She walked out of the Miami International Airport into the smothering heat of the September afternoon, inundated by the impact of another culture.

She missed the cool, exhilarating air of La Paz; the sight of the mountains jutting into the jewel-blue sky; the gentler sounds of sparser traffic; the lilting language of another people; the feeling of belonging. Though Miami teemed with activity, the sounds were too loud; the colors, too bright and glitzy; the movement, too helter-skelter, too erratic and purposeless.

She retreated into the safety of a cab and, after giving the driver the address of Garland Enterprises, attempted to collect her thoughts. She was nervous, not having seen her father for months. And their parting had been angry, hurtful. She had let him down, gone against his will, she knew he felt betrayed and rejected.

The giant glass and concrete structure that bore her father's name, loomed in the clear Miami sky. Laura emerged from the cab; paid the driver; collected her tote bag, garment bag, and purse; and stepped inside the building. The air conditioning revived her somewhat. She rode the elevator to the top floor—the floor that housed Mac's real estate offices—and, taking a deep breath, re-entered the world she had once known so well.

Everything was the same. Everything was different. There were some new faces—new office help. Her desk had been removed and two smaller ones stood in its place. The door to her father's office was closed, signaling that he was in. She passed his secretary without acknowledging her. The surprised woman rose, as if to stop Laura. But she hesitated and stood poised, torn between ritual and familiarity.

Laura entered Mac's glass and chrome office quickly. He sat at his desk, dictating into a machine. The window behind him framed his bulk. He looked up, blinked, half-rose. A fleeting look of joy crossed his face. Then it vanished. He sat down heavily and stared at her coldly, warily, through black-rimmed glasses.

"Hello, Mac," she said softly, crossing the thick, cushioned carpeting with long, purposeful strides. She stood in front of his desk for a few moments, looking at him, taking in the face, the persona of the man she'd called "father" all her life.

"Laura," he searched her eyes before adding, "I'm surprised to see you."

She wished he would reach out to hug her or even shake her hand—any physical expression. But he did not. So she sat down in the deep leather chair that always faced his desk. If it was a business meeting he wanted, she thought, then a business meeting it would be.

"How are you?" she queried. "And Mother . . . how's Mother?"

"We're both well," he said without elaborating.

"Mac," she began, groping for words. "I've missed you . . ."

"You knew where to find me," he said. There was an edge of bitterness in his voice.

She nodded and tried again. "I never wanted to hurt you. But you brought me up to be strong and independent and self-reliant. You always trained me to use my brain and make my own choices. I never rejected you. But I have to live my own life."

"In Bolivia?" he asked judgmentally.

"With God," she said, holding his eyes with a gaze of determination and honesty.

He sighed, rose from his chair, and turned to stare out the plate-glass window wall. "What do you want, Laura?"

"I just want you to listen to me," she said to his broad back. "I just want you to hear me out. If you want me to leave after that, then I will. No strings."

He crossed his arms behind him, grasping his wrist in his other hand. He said nothing, so Laura unfolded the story of Bolivia . . . of the people, their poverty, their hunger for the gospel. And finally, she revealed Michael's vision of a hospital and school for San Ramon.

At the mention of Michael, Mac whirled. "So he

182

sent you to ask for money," he accused. "For the good of Bolivia," he added sarcastically.

"No, Mac," Laura said, her own voice rising. "He didn't want me to ask you for anything. Furthermore, money isn't the problem. The Bolivians have raised their own money. The problem isn't workers. The Bolivians will supply their own work force."

Mac surveyed her skeptically. "Then what's the problem?"

Laura suppressed a smile. The businessman in him had taken over. If money wasn't the issue, what was? Sadly that was the way his mind worked. Money first.

"We seem to have run into a bureaucratic snarl," she explained. "You know, the paper-shuffling type of roadblock that has everything—the money, the people, the project—on the back burner. And until the red tape is cut, San Ramon will never have its hospital."

"What can I possibly do?" Mac asked, surprised by the direction of her request.

"Maybe nothing," she conceded. "But you know people—here, in Washington, in South America. Doesn't the daughter of some Bolivian official have a home on Gull Island?"

He nodded. "A member of their Parliament." He paced in front of the window, occasionally sending a sidelong glance at Laura. "That's it? That's all you want? All Raintree wants? A few phone calls?"

She gritted her teeth. She didn't want Michael involved. She wanted to keep things between herself and her father. "It was my idea to ask you," she told him. "My idea—and mine alone. I hoped you could help . . ." She rose, as if to leave the room.

"All right," Mac said quietly. Relief flooded her. "I'll make the calls. No promises, though, on action being taken," he warned at the look of hope on her face. "But I will call around."

She smiled at him and reached out to touch him.

But he stepped back and regarded her coolly. "After all," he said, "I owe you."

"What?" she asked, genuinely confused by his words.

"I owe you, Laura," he restated. "For Brad."

Suddenly it all became clear to her. A favor for a favor; a business deal—clean and simple. He had once tried to manipulate her into a relationship with Brad. He felt guilty about that. Making the phone calls was his way of making it up to her. Never mind that she was his daughter. Never mind that he would be helping an entire generation of people. He felt that he owed her and that now he could pay her back. After this, they would be even.

"And by the way," Mac added, absently moving some papers around on his desktop, "I do know what happened in Cannes. If it's any consolation, Brad Meyers is finished in this town."

His words left her cold and feeling a little sick at her stomach. Revenge. Mac had gotten revenge. She couldn't help wondering why. Because Brad had tried to violate her? Or because he had failed to fulfill Mac's purposes? She almost felt sorry for Brad. With Mac for an enemy, he *was* finished in Miami.

"This may take a few days," Mac said. Once more, he was all business. 'I'll get right on it. Will you be staying for a while?"

"Maybe a week. I'm not sure how long. I'd like to see Mother," she added, dreading his reaction.

Mac nodded, his voice crisp and businesslike when he spoke again. "Plan to stay at the house. I'll call ahead and let them know to expect you. And here," he added, reaching into his trouser pocket and removing a key chain. "Take my Mercedes. You know where it's parked in the lot."

She knew. In the space reserved for him. Laura reached for his car keys. She wanted to say something. Something that might break down the barrier between them. But all she could manage was a numb thank you. She took the keys, noticing that he was very careful to give them over without touching her hand.

It felt odd to be behind the wheel of a car again. With a start, Laura realized that she hadn't driven in months. In Cannes, Brad had driven. In Bolivia, she'd walked, taken a taxi or bus . . . or a plane. She remembered Theil's wrecked aircraft vividly and shuddered.

She slipped in and out of traffic effortlessly, enjoying the sight of the blue waters of the bay as she crossed over to Gull Island. At the guard house, the gatekeeper waved her through and she drove toward the white wrought-iron fence that marked off the Garland estate. In some ways, she felt that she'd been gone no longer than a day or two. So much appeared the same as when she'd left months before.

Her home was perched on the great green expanse of the clipped lawn—like a gleaming white pearl. She'd never noticed how large and impressive it was until now, as she wound up the shrubbery-lined driveway. In Bolivia, a house that size could shelter five families, she mused.

She eased the Mercedes into its berth in the four-car garage, got out, picked up her luggage, and prepared to walk up to the main house. A tarpaulin-covered hulk caught her eye. Curious, she set down her bags and crossed to the tarpaulin. She lifted it and gazed at the sleek red surface of her Thunderbird.

Mac had put the car up on blocks and covered it carefully. It was perfectly preserved and waiting for her return. She ran her hand over the supple leather upholstery. Yet all she saw in her mind's eye was Michael at the steering wheel. Michael, gunning the engine. Michael, with the wind in his tousled black hair. Quickly, she re-covered the car, picked up her bags and walked hastily to the house.

It was good to see everyone again—the maids, the cook, the gardeners. They greeted her warmly, hugging and questioning her. Ellen floated to her in a cloud of pale blue chiffon, held her tightly and told her over and over how "marvelous" she looked. They agreed that Laura would freshen up and then meet her mother on the patio for iced tea and conversation.

Laura's room was clean, immaculate, open and flooded with sunlight. She circled it fondly, touching the ceramic keepsakes, the photos, the things on the antique desk that she remembered so well. She stepped out onto her balcony overlooking the bay and watched the white-capped waves roll gently onto the glittering white sand.

Heat waves danced off the sand and left a shimmering haze across the seascape. She shut the French doors behind her and retreated into the luxurious coolness of her room.

Unpacking, she lay out her things in her private dressing room. Inez would take care of her clothes later. Laura picked up her Bible from the bottom of her tote bag. She lovingly ran her hand over its surface, remembering how it had once been fresh and new. Now, it was dog-eared, underlined, worn, and well-used, filled with Michael's interpretations of passages. Now it contained her own remarks, questions, and notations. She hugged it to herself briefly, then laid it on her desktop.

Laura sank low into the sweetly scented waters of her black marble tub, turning on the golden swan spigots whenever the water grew tepid. She dried off, relishing the thick terry towel against her body. She dressed in a silken robe, one that hung in her closet . . . waiting.

It was as if she'd never been away. Her room had been kept for her just as she had left it—clean and tidy and fresh. Her clothes had been laundered and rotated; her perfumes, powders, and colognes, neatly aligned in her bathroom. An eerie sensation of *déjà vu* flooded over her. She shivered and left her bedroom.

"You look refreshed!" her mother noted brightly as Laura joined her on the patio next to the aqua-blue pool. "I thought you might try to nap."

Laura smiled. "I lay down," she confessed. "But I couldn't sleep."

"Is something wrong?"

"I think the bed was too soft." Laura mused.

"Will you . . . be staying . . . for a while?" Ellen asked, choosing her words carefully.

"I'm not sure," Laura confessed. There was much she wanted to think about. Much she wanted to understand about herself, her feelings for Michael, for Chris. She was glad she'd come back to see her family. It suddenly occurred to her that she needed a rest—and a different perspective on her life, her future.

"You're always welcome here, Laura," Ellen said, touching her arm.

Laura smiled. "I wasn't sure. Mac didn't seem overjoyed . . ."

"He loves you, dear," Ellen assured her. "He only wants what's best for you. But it was a shock to him for you to refuse to come home with him."

"I guess it was," Laura said, nodding. "I never wanted to alienate him, you know."

"I know. But Mac isn't one to have his will crossed gracefully."

"I'm not a little child anymore."

"No . . . no, you're not."

An uneasy silence fell between them. Laura gazed out across the quiet waters of the pool and smelled the chemical aroma of chlorine rising from its rippled depths. She heard the soft, rhythmic swish of the sprinkler system in the distance. The world, this

187

world, seemed so sedate, so calm and serene; its participants, so indulged, pampered, protected. The water lapped lazily against colorful imported tiles.

"Did you know that Monica was married?" Ellen asked, interrupting Laura's meandering thoughts.

Laura gasped with surprise and focused her full attention on her mother. "Why, no!" she cried. "I had no idea . . ."

"Yes," Ellen emphasized with a wave of her hand. "An older man. Some count or duke she met over in Europe. It seems that he needed a rich American wife to bail him out of certain ancestral monetary setbacks, and she wanted a title of nobility. I guess it seemed like a fair trade-off to her at the time . . . although I know that her parents were crushed. They lost control of her ages ago . . ."

Laura shook her head. How sad. She thought of Billy and Lisa—of their wedding; of their pledge of covenant to one another. Monica didn't even know what the word meant.

"I hope it works out," Ellen said absently. "Although it seems a frivolous reason to marry. Poor Monica. She never did have much sense."

A deep feeling of melancholy stole over Laura. She stood abruptly, saying, "I think I'll try that nap now."

"Do that, dear," Ellen said with a smile. "Will you join us for dinner?"

Laura affirmed with a nod and returned to the quiet sanctity of her room.

The atmosphere at dinner was strained. She wanted to ask Mac about his promise to call and untangle the snarl of red tape surrounding Michael's project, but Mac didn't want to talk. Laura decided he didn't want to forgive, either. He left on a business trip the following morning.

Laura lazed around the house for the next few days. Her mother joined her for brief visits, sandwiched between her many social commitments. But Laura didn't mind. She needed the time alone.

She swam in the pool. She sunbathed. She went for long walks along the beach. And despite all her efforts, she remembered Michael. She saw his face in the depths of the waters. She heard him call to her in her dreams. She hungered for the reassuring guidance of his words, his piercing spiritual insights and gentle understanding. She recalled the feel of his mouth against hers; the firmness of his hands' rubbing her shoulders when she was very tired; the scent of him; the taste of him; the comfort of him. He was a part of her very fabric—interwoven and laced through all her memories. And despite Chris, he seemed to be a part of all her tomorrows.

One bright summer morning, she awoke from a brief nap beside the pool. The sun's warm rays had turned her flesh a honey-buttered gold. She rolled off the edge of the pool and submerged herself in the cool aqua waters.

She hit the surface with a sense of longing tearing at every fiber of her body, every beat of her heart. She wanted to leave this place of eternal summer. She longed to see Lisa and Billy and most of all . . . most of all . . . she longed to see Michael. She knew that it was time to go home.

## CHAPTER 12

"LAURA! YOU LOOK TERRIFIC! How good to see you again!" Lisa Powell cried as she opened her hotel room door. Laura reached out for her friend and they hugged each other enthusiastically.

It *was* good to be back. She'd taken only time enough to dump her bags in her room after arriving from the La Paz airport and had immediately gone to Lisa's room. Nervous flutterings of butterflies danced in Laura's stomach. She wanted to know everything that had happened in her two-week absence.

"Come in!" Lisa urged, pulling Laura into the hotel room. "Billy's out, but I expect him soon." She paused, pulling a chair across the floor for Laura. "I can't tell you how much I missed you," Lisa continued.

"Good grief," Laura teased good-naturedly, "You sound as if you thought I wasn't coming back."

Lisa wrinkled her turned-up nose. "*I* never doubted if for a minute."

Laura grew defensive. "You sound as if some people doubted that I would," she ventured cautiously. A strange feeling crept over her and her head started to ache as tension spread from her neck to her temples.

Lisa dropped her gaze and shrugged, "Some of us wondered . . ."

"Who?"

Lisa said nothing. Laura tried a different approach. "Was it Michael?"

Lisa reached over and took Laura's hand in hers. "You left very suddenly. You didn't call or write."

It was true. Laura pressed her temples and waited for the throbbing to stop. "Everyone knew why I left," she sighed. "Besides, there was so much I had to sort out," she finished. "Where is Michael?" she asked, almost afraid to hear the answer.

"You mean you don't know?" Lisa asked incredulously.

Laura shook her head.

"Why, your father must have fired a cannon through the Bolivian governmental hierarchy. The red tape vanished—*poof*—into thin air!" Lisa smiled and snapped her fingers for emphasis. "Michael and a small crew are in San Ramon right now, clearing off the site. They hope to get the foundation laid before the rains come. Then next winter, they can start the walls."

Laura blinked with surprise. Mac had told her nothing. In fact, he'd been out of Miami on business during her entire stay. She didn't even get to say goodbye to him, except through her mother. "So he did it," she mused, half to herself. Well, now they were even. Mac's debt to her was paid in full. "That's very good news," Laura said aloud to Lisa. She felt the sharp edge of disappointment prick her heart. She longed to see Michael. Yet, a lingering sense of foreboding filled her. Their last meeting had been strained. She wasn't sure he wanted to see her. "Anything else going on?" she asked, both to change

191

the subject and to hide her disappointment and doubts.

Lisa took a deep breath. "Chris is leaving," she added quietly, leveling her full attention at Laura. "So are Phil and Jack. Even as we speak, they're packing for the States."

Tense, her mind in turmoil, Laura stood in front of Chris's door a full five minutes before she got up the courage to knock. Her mind raced. Chris was leaving. How? Why? And what of Michael?

"Come in!" Chris called from behind the closed door. Laura screwed up her courage and, she hoped, her grace, and entered the room. The two women surveyed each other for a few moments. Chris finally turned and resumed folding her clothes. Her suitcase lay open on the bed like a yawning cave.

"Hello, Laura," she said stiffly. "Welcome back."

"Thank you." Laura felt awkward, strained. She groped for appropriate words. "It's good to be back. Miami was hot. Chris," Laura started again. "You were right about reconciling with my father. I never forgot what you told me in Magdalena and I made every effort to breach the gap between us."

Chris glanced at her. "Were you successful?"

A wry smile crossed Laura's face. "No. But the door is open. Maybe someday Mac will change his mind about me."

Chris resumed her packing. Laura's heart thumped and she dug her nails into her palms. Finally, unable to contain her curiosity any longer, she blurted, "Why are you leaving?"

"You always said the Sonshine Singers were good," Chris tossed lightly as she rummaged in her bureau for clothing. "It's time we found out how good. We're going to cut a demo tape in Nashville and circulate it to the music industry. Michael's arranged some contacts for us with old friends of his in the gospel music business." At the mention of his name,

Chris hugged a blouse to herself and stared at the wall.

Bewildered, Laura mused, "So Michael knows you're going . . ."

"Michael knows," Chris countered briskly, shaking her silken river of hair and resuming the packing process. "He thinks I have a lot to give the gospel music world."

"It's true. You have the most beautiful voice I've ever heard . . ." Laura meant it, too. Chris flipped her a half-smile, but a tight, controlled line hovered at the corners of her mouth. Laura's thoughts cried, *What else did he say to you, Chris? You've been with him much too long for nothing else to have been said!*

"I assume you'll be staying here in Bolivia?" Chris asked.

"Yes. My life is here now." Laura's answer was honest, from the deepest parts of her heart.

At that moment, Phil and Jack came bursting into the room. "Hey, Billy's got a taxi waiting. You'd better get moving . . ." Jack started. "Laura!" he hailed as soon as he saw her. "Have you heard the news? Isn't it great?"

Laura smiled warmly at Jack's beaming, little-boy enthusiasm. "It's great," she confirmed. "But we'll miss all of you."

Chris quickly completed her packing while Laura, Jack, and Phil made small talk. When she was finished, the men took her things and walked to the elevator. "One last look!" she called to them as they stepped inside.

"Well, don't take all day!" Phil warned with exasperation. Then, they were gone and only Laura and Chris stood alone in the hall. Chris rechecked the room and finally went to the elevator herself. The two women stood silently, waiting for the car to arrive.

There was so much Laura wanted to know. So much she wished she could say. But the wall was there—the wall that Chris had always kept between them. When the elevator doors opened, Chris stepped inside and held the door. "Coming?"

"No . . ." Laura said. "I-I'll walk down to my floor. I-I need the exercise . . ." Even to her own ears, her comment sounded weak and silly.

"You know, Laura," Chris said awkwardly. "I-I didn't always treat you . . . like a Christian . . . should have . . ." Her words came hesitantly. "I . . . want you to know . . . I never hated you."

"I know," Laura told her, a little too quickly. *It was just that you loved Michael* . . . she finished in her mind. She wanted to reach out to Chris, to embrace the homeless, hurt little girl locked within. But she did not. Instinctively Laura knew that Chris belonged to Christ and that He would mend her heart in His time. In His way.

The elevator doors slid shut. Laura stood, her heart numb, in front of the painted metal doors, listening to the elevator hum as it descended, taking Chris Avery out of her life forever.

"*Vaya con Dios*, Chris . . ." she whispered into the empty hallway. "Go with God."


"Michael wants to see you." Billy's words ran through Laura's mind over and over. "As soon as possible, Michael wants to see you." After Chris had left, Laura had gone to her room and fallen into an exhausted sleep. Hours later, the knocking on her door had roused her. She'd risen, feeling drugged, and opened her door to Billy and Lisa. "Michael wants to see you," had been the message.

"But Michael's in San Ramon," she'd said, struggling to focus her thoughts, fighting her way out of her sleep stupor.

"Then we'll fly into San Ramon tomorrow," Billy had said matter-of-factly. The thought of getting back into a little single-engine plane sent chills through her, but she'd nodded her consent. Michael wanted to see her. And more than anything, *she* wanted to see Michael.

Now, bouncing along in the Jeep from the dirt airstrip to the far side of San Ramon where the site for the hospital was being cleared, Laura could scarcely control the hammering of her heart. The driver concentrated on keeping the vehicle on the rutted dirt road. Laura watched, gripping the seat and the roll bar, as the village scooted past them on either side. They passed Inga Swensen's house and Laura remembered poignantly the day they had spent with her. She remembered the plane crash, the days and nights in the wilderness. She recalled her fear, her loneliness, her reliance on God. He had sustained her. Through all of it, He had been her source of strength.

She saw the partial clearing through the dusty windshield of the Jeep. A group of men were working, methodically eliminating the dense jungle growth under the intense midday sun. Their great machetes swung back and forth across the green tangle of brush and palmettos, slicing and leveling everything in their paths. Long, curved, silver blades glinting in the sun, flashing and singing as they swept across the enormous site.

Once the land was cleared, they would start a fire. A controlled, yet consuming fire that would burn off the remainder of the growth. It would leave the clearing black and barren and ready for building. She tried to imagine a structure there and could not. All she could see were the huge sweeping machetes, hacking, cutting, leveling.

And she saw Michael. He, too, worked in the partially cleared land site. He was dressed in jeans, stripped to his waist, a red bandanna wound around his forehead. He swung a machete rhythmically from side to side, the muscles rippling across his back and arms as the blade descended.

195

He looked up as the Jeep approached and squinted into the bright sun. She got out of the vehicle and took a few small steps forward. Recognizing her, Michael stopped in midswing. He turned, drove the blade deep into the trunk of a small tree, and came bounding toward her.

He closed the gap between them in a few loping strides. He grabbed her, picked her off the ground, and whirled her around, laughing. He bent his head and kissed her fully on the lips. He tasted salty and warm and she tingled from his touch, gasping for breath as his arms held her in a steel grip.

"You're here!" he shouted.

Laura, overwhelmed by his greeting, stammered in confusion. "Well, of course I'm here . . ."

Michael set her down and eagerly led her away from the curious glances of the workers. So dense was the surrounding jungle, that in only a few yards, they seemed completely alone. Vines snaked from overhead trees, and thickets of growth muffled the work party. He captured her again, locking his fingers together across the small of her back. Perspiration glistened on his bare shoulders, pooling in the hair on his chest. His skin stretched, bronzed and taut, over firm, hard muscles. A trickle of moisture traveled down his neck, his chest, over his lean, flat stomach.

"I've missed you," he told her. His violet-blue eyes glowed with ardor, singeing her heart, igniting her old hunger for him. He pulled her closer. She felt the dampness of his chest soak through her shirt, as his mouth touched hers. She grew dizzy from the love she was feeling for him.

She withdrew from his embrace and stepped backward. She couldn't think straight with him so near. And she had so many questions.

Michael spoke first. "You were right about your father's ability to help get the project off the ground. Thank you."

Grateful? Was that what he was feeling toward her?

"You're a remarkable woman, Laura." His voice was low, husky. His mouth formed her name, caressing the syllables, and she felt bonded to him, to the fire that simmered beneath his surface.

"It was the least I could do," she whispered.

"You've got courage and character and mettle. You'll need them out here."

Her heart hammered. What was he saying? "I-I guess we all have our work cut out for us," she offered. "I mean with the Singers gone and everything."

Michael brought his hand to her face and laid his palm against her cheek. His voice, deep and rich, lured her back into the pool of his eyes. "I was very obtuse about Chris," he confessed. "And about her feelings."

*So they had talked about more than Chris's singing career!*

Michael slid his hand behind Laura's neck and ever so slowly drew her closer to him. "I respected her. I admired her. I was grateful for her. But I never loved her. She was nothing more to me than a sister in the Lord. Do you understand?"

Laura felt herself trembling, captured by the spell of his words. "What do you want me to do, Michael?"

"Come with me. . ."

"Where?"

He caught her hand in his hand and brought it to his lips. "Wherever I go."

"Of course, I will . . ." she said, still confused, not seeing his purposes. "All you ever had to do was ask me."

"Laura," he said, pulling the words from his deepest interiors. "Don't you see? I couldn't ask before. You were a princess. You lived in a palace. You had everything money could buy. How could I ask you to give all that up for . . . this?" He gestured

197

at the jungle surrounding them. "I had nothing to give you."

Her pulse raced. "None of it mattered, Michael. None of it!" she cried passionately. "When I was away, in Miami, I felt so . . ." she groped for words. ". . . lonely. I drove my sports car and thought of you. I walked the beach and thought of you. I sat in my room and I thought of you. Did you really think I wouldn't come back?" Her voice held an accusing, hurt tone.

He chose his words carefully. "I knew you would come if I asked you. But you had to come because God asked you. You had to come for His sake . . . not for mine. Laura,"—he paused and raised his arm in a sweeping gesture—"this is my life. This is all I will ever have. This is all I will ever be."

"What do you want?" she asked. The staccato beat of her heart crescendoed against her ribcage.

"I want you," he said simply. "For all time. I love you. I think I've loved you since that first time I saw you in the park, all dressed in red. Marry me, Laura . . . stay with me."

For Laura, time stood still. The hushed, hot jungle air closed in on her. Somewhere overhead a wild parrot screeched and fluttered in the trees. She lifted her eyes again to Michael's face, not quite daring to breathe.

She saw his heart . . . saw his love in the mirror of his eyes. It was true—Michael loved her. She gave her answer by slipping into his arms. She raised on her toes, arching to meet his kiss. Michael's mouth came down on hers, warm and soft and loving.

## EPILOGUE

The rain fell in the Bolivian night, across the village compound, turning the dirt streets into rivers of mud. It beat steadily, warm and cleansing, constant, with a droning sound that blocked out all other noise from the surrounding jungle. The small mission church glowed with the light from a hundred candles, their flames flickering and dancing, untouched by the drumming, drenching rain outside.

For the people sitting inside the church, the walls offered a cocoon of protection while the rhythm of the rain created an aura of contentment—a cushion against the inexorable movement of the age-old seasons.

In the wooden pews, Theil, Helga, and Inga Swensen sat with Enrique, Mara and her family, and visiting friends from the Mission of La Paz. At the front of the church, Rey Ortiz stood on the steps of the altar, facing the tightly-knit congregation. Lisa Powell, gowned in a simple dress of hand-loomed linen, clutched a nosegay of flowers and waited breathlessly at Rey's side.

A lone guitarist played as the congregation sat hushed, expectant. Michael Raintree stepped forward, towering, darkly handsome, next to Rey. From the back of the church, down the smooth stone aisle, Laura came, on the arm of Billy Powell, with measured steps.

She floated in the candlelight, a vision in lace and satin and tulle. Her eyes never left Michael's and he urged her toward him, in silent coded promises . . . man to woman. She did not see the people as she glided past them to take her place beside Michael. She rather sensed their presence, feeling their love reach out and wrap around her. Her telegram home had been unanswered. It didn't matter.

Laura took her place at Michael's side, fastening her sight on the gleaming cross that stood on the altar, burnished, radiant, resplendent with the light from the surrounding candles. Michael took her hand, placing it gently over his arm. She peered up at him through the haze of her veil and read his message of covenant love in the intensity of his gaze.

He removed two candles from the altar cloth. One, he gave to Laura. The other, he lit from the candle that already burned and shimmered beside the golden cross. He cupped his hand protectively around the struggling tiny flame until it caught, and grew long and bright and strong. He waited until he was sure it would not go out.

Then he lowered the yellow flame of his candle to the unlit wick of Laura's. The tapers met. And as the lifeless wick of her candle touched the glowing flame of his, it leaped upward in a blaze of brilliance. For a moment the flames merged into a solitary stream. Rising together, in the cleansed moist night air, they burned in a dazzling luminescent union. One eternal flame.

## ABOUT THE AUTHOR

LURLENE MCDANIEL, a former owner of an advertising agency, has pursued a career as a freelance writer for the past seventeen years. She is the author of thirteen books prior to ETERNAL FLAME—her first work of romantic fiction—and continues to write advertising copy and perform voice-overs for TV and radio commercial and promotional spots. She has taught courses in advertising copywriting.

She and her husband, Joe, live in Lutz, Florida, with their two sons.

# A Letter To Our Readers

Dear Reader:

Pioneering is an exhilarating experience, filled with opportunities for exploring new frontiers. The Zondervan Corporation is proud to be the first major publisher to launch a series of inspirational romances designed to inspire and uplift as well as to provide wholesome entertainment. In order that we might better contribute to your reading enjoyment, we would appreciate your taking a few minutes to respond to the following questions and return to:

Anne Severance, Editor
Serenade/Serenata Books
1415 Lake Drive, S.E.
Grand Rapids, Michigan 49506

1. Did you enjoy reading ETERNAL FLAME?

☐ Very much. I would like to see more books by this author!
☐ Moderately
☐ I would have enjoyed it more if _____

2. Where did you purchase this book? _____

3. What influenced your decision to purchase this book?

☐ Cover      ☐ Back cover copy
☐ Title      ☐ Friends
☐ Publicity      ☐ Other _____

4. Please rate the following elements from 1 (poor) to 10 (superior).

☐ Heroine      ☐ Plot
☐ Hero      ☐ Inspirational theme
☐ Setting      ☐ Secondary characters

5. Which settings would you like to see in future Serenade/Serenata Books?

_____      _____

_____      _____

6. What are some inspirational themes you would like to see treated in future books?

_____      _____

_____      _____

7. Would you be interested in reading other Serenade/Serenata or Serenade/Saga Books?

☐ Very interested
☐ Moderately interested
☐ Not interested

8. Please indicate your age range:

☐ Under 18      ☐ 25–34      ☐ 46–55
☐ 18–24      ☐ 35–45      ☐ Over 55

9. Would you be interested in a Serenade book club? If so, please give us your name and address:

Name _____

Occupation _____

Address _____

City _____ State _____ Zip _____

*Serenade/Serenata Books* are inspirational romances in contemporary settings, designed to bring you a joyful, heart-lifting reading experience.

Other Serenade books available in your local book-store:

Watch for these Serenade Books in the months to come: